TOPZ SECRET DIARIES

SARAH'S SECRET SCRIBBLINGS

Alexa Tewkesbury

D1322227

For a list of our National Distributors visit our website
www.cwr.org.uk

Concept development, editing, design and production
by CWR.

Illustrations: Helen Reason, Dan Donovan and CWR
Printed in Finland by Bookwell
ISBN: 978-1-85345-432-5

Hi, I'm Sarah.

Thanks for picking up my diary. You're about to uncover the whole zany truth about me and my wacky world! There's stuff about my twin brother, John (and what could be wackier than living with him?), my soppy cat, Saucy, who's a total cuddle freak – and, of course, I natter on about what I get up to with the rest of the Topz Gang. Being one of the Gang is the coolest! You can read all about us on the next page if you don't already know who we are.

You'll soon see that I've been learning loads about God. For instance, did you know that, even when it doesn't feel like it, God is ALWAYS there? It doesn't matter what we want to talk about with Him, He's never too busy to listen. Fantasticoco, or what?!

So, go on! Snuggle up with my secret scribblings and take a peep at life the way I see it. Have fun!

HI! WE'RE THE TOPZ GANG

– Topz because we all live at the 'top' of something …
either in houses at the top of the hill, at the top of the
flats by the park, even sleeping in a top bunk counts!
We are all Christians, and we go to Holly Hill School.

We love Jesus, and try to work out our faith in God
in everything we do – at home, at school and with our
friends. That even means trying to show God's love to
the Dixons Gang who tend to be bullies, and can be a
real pain!

If you'd like to know more about us, visit our website
at **www.cwr.org.uk/topz**. You can read all about us,
and how you can get to know and understand the Bible
more by reading our 'Topz' notes, which are great fun,
and written every two months just for you!

DIPPY

MONDAY, 16 NOVEMBER
After school

John just called me dippy. HE can talk! Does he really think I don't know that he sings to snails and has the world's biggest collection of empty crisp packets stuffed into four shoeboxes under his bed? I asked Mum once what he wanted them for. She said she wasn't sure but it was probably just a phase. So I pointed out that perhaps she ought to stop him because eating lots of crisps is a serious health hazard (we've just finished doing nutrition in science so I know these things). But Mum said that as I'd just had four chocolate Hobnobs and an entire Galaxy Kingsize, I couldn't really comment.

Then she put on one of her wise faces and added, 'Anyway, imagine what a boring place the world would be if we only enjoyed collecting sensible things.'

Mum, I thought, imagine what a nutritional nightmare the world would be if we all collected empty crisp packets.

Only now John's calling ME dippy when all I'm doing is wanting to be on my own in my bedroom so I can write my diary. Just because he never wants to do anything on <u>his</u> own. I was dying to say, 'At least I don't collect used crisp packets,' but that would have meant having a full-on fall out and I didn't think I had the energy. John said, 'What do you want to be on your own for?'

'Because I've got things to do,' I told him.

'Like what?' he asked.

'Oh, you know,' I answered, 'stuff.'

'What stuff?' he went on.

'Just stuff, all right?' I said. Can't a girl have any secrets in her own house?

'So, give me an example!' he shouted up the stairs after me.

Brothers! They just can't let things drop, can they? Are they all as annoying?

Louise (new leader at Sunday Club) would understand. But then, she's a girl. Well, a lady. She's the one who started me off keeping a diary in the first place. She says it's a great way to keep track of what's going on in your life. She also says if you've got problems, writing them down can sometimes help you sort them out. (It hasn't helped me to sort out John yet but maybe I haven't been writing it for long enough.) Louise says she's always writing in hers. She says when she looks back over it she can see how God's answered her prayers – even if the answer wasn't what she was expecting.

I like Louise. She has to wear glasses when she's reading otherwise she says the words go all blurred and foggy. I've tried screwing up my eyes to see if I can make everything go blurred and foggy but I can still see perfectly well. (I know I'm strange.)

SCREAM!!!

Just had a MAJOR interruption from John. Now I can't think what I was on about! Why do brothers always have to do that? I mean, interrupt you when you're trying to get on with something REALLY important? He asked what I was doing that was so secret and said he'd start playing ping-pong against my bedroom door if I didn't tell him. Honestly! How am I supposed to have any sort of life? I ended up blurting it out just to make him go away. I said I was writing a diary like Louise only he'd never get to read it because it was private. He said he wouldn't want to read a load of girly stuff anyway. Then he said why was I bothering because my life was about as interesting as watching Mum do the hoovering?

That's when I threw my hairbrush at him and he called Mum because it hit him on the elbow. Then Mum made ME say sorry! I told her he'd started it. But she just said we had to be kind to each other and that throwing hairbrushes at people never solved anything. I didn't actually MEAN it to hit him.

And now Mum's calling up that supper's on the table so I've got to go and eat – CAN YOU BELIEVE IT? There's something really important going on that I need to write about and no one'll leave me alone long enough to do it!

TUESDAY, 17 NOVEMBER
Morning. Got up late (as usual)

Ran out of writing time yesterday, because after supper I had to finish some colouring for history. We're doing this thing on the Elizabethans. I've drawn a picture of Elizabeth I in all her snazzy queen gear which, amazingly, Mrs Parker wants to put up on the wall. Then John wanted me to fill in a quiz sheet he's doing for maths about hobbies. (I did wonder if this was the right time to mention that I know about his crisp packet collection, but decided against it.) Then I had to do my reading. Then it was bedtime.

Sometimes trying to get five minutes to yourself in this house is like trying to climb a mountain with your hands tied behind your back.

Anyway, can't stop now. Mum's calling. Got to go and have breakfast or I'll be late for school.

Same day. After school

John's round at Benny's. FINALLY I get some peace. At least it would be peaceful if I had the faintest clue what's going on. This has been the worst day. It's the new girl, Gemma. She's only been at our school since the beginning of term. Her parents moved here from Scotland in the summer holidays and she didn't know anybody. But we'd just been looking at Matthew's Gospel in Sunday Club (the bit where Jesus talks about loving other people as much as we love ourselves – Matthew 22 verse 39, we had to learn it), and I thought this was a good opportunity to give it a go. Being loving, that is. So I said to Mrs Parker that I'd sit next to Gemma and look after her and everything.

Actually it was easy because we got on really well. We both love animals and I said she'd have to come over and meet my cat, Saucy, and John's dog, Gruff. She said she was going to get a hamster soon and I could come round to her house and see it. We both like literacy more than numeracy. Also, she's BRILLIANT at drawing. I'm only sort of OK, but she said she'd always help me out. Mrs Parker was REALLY impressed with our joint castle painting – we got a Head Teacher's star for it.

Gemma said I'd made starting at a new school easy. She hadn't felt like a freak for being the only one who didn't know anybody. Everything was groovy-doovy with us, it really was.

Until bonfire night.

Mum and Dad always take John and me to the big display in the park. Gemma said she'd definitely be there, so I told her I'd look out for her. Then HER mum and dad could meet MY mum and dad and all that.

But Gemma never came. I looked and looked but I'm sure she wasn't there. In the end I spent most of the time mucking about with my friend Josie so it was good fun anyway, I suppose.

But when I saw Gemma at school the next day, all I said was, 'Where did you get to last night?' and she gave me a filthy look and said, 'Mind your own business!' I tried to ask her if she was all right. But she just said for me to leave her alone and that she'd never asked me to be her friend in the first place.

Then she was off school the whole of the next week. I thought perhaps she was ill and that's why she'd been grumpy. I asked Mrs Parker if she knew what was wrong but all she said was that Gemma would be back next Monday.

And then she didn't come back on Monday (yesterday), she came back today. I tried to be all, 'Hello! Feeling better?' You know, pretend nothing's happened so we could get back to normal – but she pretty well blanked me. It was like that all day. And now we're not even sitting together because she asked Mrs Parker if she could move nearer the window. Mrs Parker said, 'Yes, if you'd be more comfortable!' I MEAN, HONESTLY! 'YES, IF YOU'D BE MORE COMFORTABLE'!! If I asked to sit by the window she'd tell me to stop wasting time and go and finish my work!

And the worst of it all is I DON'T KNOW WHAT I'M SUPPOSED TO HAVE DONE. God wants us to be kind to people and I've been kind! I've made Gemma feel really at home, I know I have. It's so unfair.

Bedtime

Not sleepy. Josie came round earlier. She's doing a diary too. She says we ought to have a race to see who finishes their notebook first. It'll probably be Josie – her writing's bigger than mine.

She asked how it was going with Gemma (she knows she's fallen out with me). I said I couldn't understand it because all I'd tried to do was be nice to her. Then Josie said why didn't I try praying for her? (Josie can be like that. All sort of sensible and knowing.)

She said, 'Even though you can't work out what's going on, God knows all about it. Ask Him to help sort it for you.'

I said, 'But it's really hard praying for someone who's

upset you.'

'I know,' she answered (sensibly and knowingly), 'but lots of people upset Jesus and He still prayed for them. Sometimes you've just got to do it anyway.'

The trouble is, I don't want to. So even if I do pray for Gemma, I can't see God answering a prayer that I don't really mean. Why does life have to be so complicated?

Then Josie said, 'If you're going to find it that difficult, ask God to help you talk to Him. He can do that too.'

Now I come to think of it, sometimes talking to Josie can be a bit like talking to Louise.

Oh help. It's no good, I'm going to have to do it. Maybe if I write it down it'll make it easier. Louise says it helps writing things down. (Not sure how. It hasn't helped so far.)

Here goes...

Dear Lord God,
Sorry, sorry, sorry! I'm sorry I don't feel like praying for Gemma. I'm sorry I'm really angry with her. I'm sorry I don't think I mean what I'm saying! I want to mean it but she's really upset me. I thought I'd made a good friend but it's all gone wrong. How can you want to do something nice for someone when they've made you feel bad?

I know You still prayed for the people who let You down, Jesus. But it's just so hard. Please help sort out what's wrong between Gemma and me. And if it is my fault, help me to know how to put things right.

And please look after Gemma. I really do want You to, even though it feels as if I don't.

I wonder if God ever has trouble making sense of our prayers. Probably not. He wants us to talk to Him. So I suppose even when what we say is a garbled load of mish-mash, He still gets the general idea.

Mum says lights off. Awwww! I haven't finished. Not nearly. More tomorrow.

WEDNESDAY, 18 NOVEMBER
4.10pm

Got up really late and nearly missed the bus. I was awake for hours in the night because I couldn't stop thinking about Gemma. Then, just when I finally got to sleep because I found a really comfy way to lie (on my tummy with both hands under my pillow), Saucy jumped up on the bed and started bouncing about on the back of my neck! Typical! It wouldn't have been so bad if she'd had her claws tucked in. But she didn't and they're really sharp. I woke up thinking I'd got my hairbrush stuck down my nightie.

Saucy, it's a good job I love you, that's all I can say! But I do sometimes wonder why you can't be normal. I thought cats were supposed to be out all night, prowling around and digging old fish bones out of people's bins. Not Saucy. She'd rather be indoors trying to jam herself inside my pillowcase.

I suppose it's quite sweet really. It's just that once I was awake all I could think about was Gemma again ... which meant I couldn't get to sleep again ... which meant tossing and turning trying to find another super-comfy position again ... otherwise it would be morning again and I'd have had no sleep at all!

I tried lying on my back with my hands under my pillow. But when Saucy plonked herself down next to my head, her tail flopped onto my face. I spent the next half an hour picking hairs off my tongue. I'm sure I haven't got them all even now.

Next thing I knew, Mum was yelling up the stairs that it was five minutes until the bus came. She said if I didn't get up right away I'd have to go to school in my nightie – I wasn't having the day off just because I couldn't be bothered to get out of bed! I asked why she hadn't woken me earlier and she said she had – twice! I don't remember her waking me. I just hoped this was all part of a very bad dream. In a moment I'd wake up and realise I was still asleep because it wasn't really morning at all. (Not sure that makes sense but I think I know what I mean.)

Anyway, is it my fault we have a cat with NITS – Nearly Impossible To stop Snuggling? (I didn't have time to go into this with Mum. I just had to grab a couple of muesli bars and run.)

There's one good thing, though. It was all such a mad panic, I forgot about Gemma until we were nearly at school. And forgetting about Gemma for five minutes turned out to be the nicest thing to happen all day.

Josie was away (which I can't understand because how can she be ill when she seemed fine yesterday evening?). So I ended up having to work with Tom Gray in numeracy, and he's REALLY irritating. I know I'm not supposed to feel that way about anyone because God wants us to love everybody. But it's almost impossible with Tom Gray. He's forever doing stuff like sticking rubbers down the back of your jumper and pinching your pencil case.

He also does this pathetic Irish voice thing (his mum comes from Ireland). If you ask him a question, he just sits there tickling his chin and saying, 'To be sure, to be sure, to be sure' over and over until you wished you'd never asked him anything in the first place. I bet even Jesus would have felt annoyed if one of His disciples had kept on muttering, 'To be sure, to be sure' all the time He was trying to explain a parable or something.

Of course we didn't get the work sheet done, so Mrs Parker kept us in at morning break. We had to finish it then. She also said that if Tom and I couldn't do better than this, she probably wouldn't let us work together again … I suppose there are some things to be thankful for.

After supper

Josie rang. She's got tonsillitis and she sounds really bad – sort of croaky and feeble. She said when she woke up this morning she thought she had a brick down her throat. She went to the doctor. He said she could either have this totally disgusting yellow medicine or she could have tablets. But Josie said she didn't fancy trying to get a lumpy tablet down her throat past the brick that was already in there. So she'd gone for the disgusting medicine, and it truly was – disgusting, that is.

I told her what an awful day I'd had, especially in PE. We were doing ball stuff in the hall and Mrs Parker chose two captains to pick teams. I hate it when she does that anyway – I'm nearly always one of the last to get picked. But this time one of the captains was Tom Gray (who obviously wasn't going to want me on his team because he said it was MY fault he'd lost his morning break), and the other one was Gemma. Talk about having no hope! I tried smiling at Gemma a few times while she was choosing. But she just carried on ignoring me like she'd been doing all day.

So, of course, at the end it was just me left. Mrs Parker told me to join Tom's side. From the look he gave me, I'm sure he'd rather have watched my legs drop off than have me on his team.

Josie said she was sorry and she'd be back at school soon, but then she started feeling sick so she had to go and lie down.

I don't understand it. I read through that prayer I wrote yesterday. It hasn't made any difference. Nothing's changed. If anything, it's got worse. All I can think is that God's got a lot on and isn't able to listen to me at the moment. Surely He'd have sorted things out if He'd heard me. In a minute I'll ask Him to help Josie get better. Hopefully He'll hear me then.

7.20pm
John just called me grumpy guts. He said if I didn't stop frowning I'd get lines so deep I'd end up looking like one of those dogs with the wrinkly faces. I told him I'd wrinkle HIS face if he didn't leave me alone.

Bedtime (again)
Mum's been having a long chat. She said she was sorry she shouted this morning because I didn't get up. She said, if there was something wrong, why didn't I just tell her about it? So I told her about Gemma and my triple awful day and she gave me a big cuddle.

She said, 'Why don't you leave Gemma alone for a bit? There could be lots of reasons why she's being off with you.'

I said, 'Yes, but I've talked to God about it. It doesn't seem to have done any good. I don't think He's listening.'

She said, 'Sometimes you have to be really patient. God hears all our prayers but He doesn't always answer them straight away. And when He does answer them, it isn't always in the way we're expecting.'

I said, 'But it's really hard being patient when you want something so much. And I really want Gemma to be my friend again.'

'I know you do,' Mum said. 'Give it time.'

(Mum also said I ought to sleep with my bedroom

door shut tonight so Saucy doesn't disturb me. Can't do that, though. Saucy's got NITS and she needs my pillowcase.)

I love my mum.

THURSDAY, 19 NOVEMBER
(Morning – five minutes to bus)
Off again. Today just can't be as bad as yesterday … can it? Please let Josie be back at school.

Just got home
Josie wasn't at school. Messed about with Paul and John at lunchtime. Don't normally do that with John but he was being worryingly kind to me this morning. I think Mum must have told him to be nice.

Later
Don't know the time exactly. The battery in my clock must have died because it's telling me it's 2.00, which can't be right. At 2.00 this afternoon I was working on that thing for our class assembly next week. We all had to pick someone from our family and write a paragraph about them. Mrs Parker says she'll choose her ten favourite ones to be read out for the assembly (which obviously is going to be about families). I was going to do mine about Mum. But then I decided to write about John. We'd just been playing football and I'd got four goals past him and he hadn't got cross! Normally he hates it when I do that.

Anyway, I was just trying to think of something nice to write about him when I saw Mrs Parker go over to Gemma and put her arm round her. Gemma had her head right down. Mrs Parker asked her if she wanted to go and sit quietly in the library. Gemma must have nodded (I couldn't really see with Mrs Parker all over her) because then she got up and went out. Everyone was sort of looking at each other and I felt really bad. If Gemma had still been friends with me, she might have asked if I could go with her. Then maybe I could have helped.

I put up my hand. I know Mum says I should leave Gemma alone but I couldn't sit there and do nothing. Mrs Parker didn't see straight away and when she did she sounded a bit annoyed.

'Yes, Sarah?'

I said, 'Shall I go and sit with Gemma?'

Mrs Parker said (well, snapped really), 'Gemma's absolutely fine. All she needs is a bit of peace. Come on, back to work, everyone. I want this finished this afternoon.' And that was that.

But Gemma wasn't absolutely fine. She didn't come back into class. I think she went home.

I don't know what's up but something definitely is. So I've made a decision. I'm not going to ask God for us to be friends again. Instead, I'm going to ask Him to be Gemma's friend and help her sort out what's wrong. He's bound to know what it is. If anyone can help her, He can.

Even later
Rang Josie. She won't be back at school tomorrow.

I said I'd pray for her again. She said thank you and said she knew someone had been praying because she was beginning to get used to the yellow medicine. She didn't feel as though just the sight of it would make her throw up any more.

Bedtime now. Getting a headache for some reason. Probably the thought of the yellow medicine. My clock now says 2.25. Mmm. Must remember to ask Mum for a new battery.

FRIDAY (YUKDAY), 20 NOVEMBER

Really bad night last night. Nothing to do with Saucy though. I just woke up loads. First I was too hot, then I was too cold. Then my throat seemed to swell up to at least 50 times its normal size. I could hardly manage to swallow. And when I did swallow, I wished I hadn't because it hurt so much. My head felt as if someone was bashing it with a rounders bat – from the inside – and then my tummy started too.

This morning Mum said I looked awful and when she took my temperature it was 102° or something.

She said, 'No school. I'm ringing the doctor.'

Turns out I've got tonsillitis.

'I expect I got it from my friend, Josie,' I croaked, feebly.

Dr Forbes-Watkins just said, 'Ah, there's a lot of it about.' But he didn't say it was Josie's fault or anything, he just went and printed off a prescription for Josie's disgusting yellow medicine. He didn't even ask if I'd rather have tablets.

When we got home I was sick (I hadn't tried the medicine yet. I just felt really ill in the car) so I went back to bed.

Later

Just rang Josie to thank her for sharing her brick with me. I know where it came from even if Dr F-W won't admit it. All I can say is UUUUUURRRRGHHH! Must lie down. Can't remember when I felt this bad. And to call that medicine disgusting doesn't even come close to describing its disgustingness.

SATURDAY MORNING, 21 NOVEMBER

Still feel UUUUUURRRRGHHH! John says I look UUUUUURRRRGHHH too. He's only had a quick peep, though. Mum and Dad have told him to keep away so he doesn't catch anything. But he reckons the whole house is probably full of my germs anyway. If we could see them I bet they'd look really ugly. All green and slimy with red eyes and slobbery mouths. And they'd all be laughing their heads off because any minute now it'll be time for another two tongue-curdling spoonfuls of Dr F-W's yellow death juice. I'm sure the way this medicine works is that you <u>force</u> yourself to get better as quickly as possible so that you can stop taking it.

Not sure what the time is – keep forgetting about batteries

It's very boring just lying here but I can't be bothered to do much else. I'd been praying for Gemma but I think I may have gone to sleep in the middle so I'm going to do it again. I want God to help her not to get tonsillitis. If Dr F-W's right and there is a lot of it about, I think she's probably got enough to cope with without having to go through the yellow death juice ordeal as well.

Getting dark

I must have been asleep for hours, because last time I can remember actually thinking anything, it was broad daylight.

Mum just brought me up a drink. I'm supposed to have lots of 'fluids'. Why is it that whenever you're ill, people stop saying 'water' or 'juice' and start calling everything you drink 'fluids'? If I said, 'Please may I have some fluids,' whenever I was thirsty, I bet I'd get some really strange looks.

Might be worth trying ...

Anyway, while I was gulping down my <u>fluids,</u> I finally remembered to ask Mum for another clock battery, and guess what? She hasn't got one.

Probably the middle of the night

It's very quiet. I wonder if time passes more slowly when you haven't got a clue what the time actually is …

Sort of daylight

I think that was probably the worst night's sleep I've ever had – mostly because I've been awake for nearly all of it. When I did fall asleep (about twice for about two minutes each time), I had really weird dreams. One of them had this strange sort of caterpillar thing in it that seemed to be living under John's bed. He didn't mind it being there but Mum got a bit upset about it when she went to put his empty crisp packets in the washing machine … Freaky, or what! I'm beginning to think there's more to tonsillitis than Dr F-W's letting on. Must remember to compare dreams with Josie tomorrow.

SUNDAY MORNING (AT LAST), 22 NOVEMBER

Dad's just been in with some toast and my first slurp of the day of yellow death juice. The worrying thing is I almost enjoyed the death juice more than the toast (what is happening to me?). I've never eaten soggy cardboard soaked in vinegar. But for some reason that's all I could think of when I tried to chew my way through a slice. Dad said I was making very weird faces and would I rather have had bran flakes?

I said, 'Not really, thanks.'

He said, 'Never mind, poppet, just make sure you drink plenty of <u>fluids</u>.'

You see? That word again.

So I said, <u>very</u> deliberately, 'Yes, Dad. Next time you come up, please could you bring me some more blackcurrant and apple fluid?'

Rather disappointingly, he just smiled and said, 'Of course I will, poppet.'

Lunchtime – ish

Mum decided to do a cooked lunch today. She doesn't usually because it's too late to start cooking when we get back from church. But, of course, we couldn't go today because of my fiendish tonsil fever. I wasn't really hungry but Dad said she'd spent ages 'slaving over a hot stove' so I thought I ought to have a roast potato.

That's when I realised I was beginning to feel a bit better. My throat still thinks Saucy's been using it to sharpen her claws on. But I haven't felt sick today and my headache's almost gone.

One roast potato was more than enough, though.

5.30pm (Borrowed Mum's watch)

Yay! Cool afternoon. Josie's been over. She rang
after lunch to say she was lots better. She said, could
she come round and keep me company while I was
moping about on my sick bed? (Her mum said it was
fine because we were probably sharing the same bugs
anyway.) I told her I wasn't moping about. She said,
'Good, because I've had a great idea and it won't work
if you're still all weak and feeble.'

When she got here she asked, 'What fantastic
opportunity does laying in bed for hours give you?'

To be honest I couldn't think of anything – which
Josie was really pleased about because she wanted it to
be her idea. So she grinned all over her face and said,
'Deciding how to give your bedroom a makeover!'

Nope, I'd never have thought of that in a million
years. But Josie was really excited about it. So I smiled
(as much as I could anyway, given that my throat feels
like the roof of my mouth does when I burn it on a
chip) and tried to look really pleased.

Next thing I knew, she was waving a piece of paper
under my nose and saying, 'Look, I've made a checklist.'

If there's one thing I've learned about Josie it's that
when she starts making lists, you know she's DEADLY
serious.

'Right. Colour,' she said.

'What do you mean?' I asked.

'What colour do you want your room to be?'

'I quite like it the colour it is,' I said, pretty feebly
really. All this excitement was wearing me out.

'Yes, I know,' Josie went on, 'but if you could have
your walls any colour in the whole world, what would
it be?'

I could see I was going to have to start thinking (not easy when you've been lying in bed for nearly three days and your brain seems to have turned into a slab of fruit cake). So I tried to remember every colour I'd ever seen and then said, 'Turquoise.'

Josie raised her eyebrows a bit but she wrote it down anyway.

'Next question,' she went on. 'Where would you like your bed to be?'

I thought, Josie, I don't know whether you've noticed but this is a REALLY small room. With a built-in cupboard along one wall, the window in the one next to it and my door in another, there isn't much of a choice where you put stuff.

She could see I was struggling with that one so we moved on.

By the time we'd got through Josie's checklist, she told me I'd decided on:

a turquoise bedroom
yellow curtains with blue and green stripes
a bed with one of those floaty canopy things over it (purple in this case)
a fluffy white carpet and a Tigger rug
a pink chest of drawers
a self-tidying bookcase
on one wall: a framed photo of the Topz Gang winning last summer's inter-church cycle race for Africa
on another wall: a picture of Saucy lying upside down in the ironing basket

a small storage box to slide under the bed containing a sensible supply of emergency chocolate (Josie said please could I include a few Snickers bars for when she came over because sometimes she had emergencies too)
a giant orange beanbag in the corner with 'SARAH'S GIANT ORANGE BEANBAG' stitched on it in red.

I also quite liked the idea of a fishy theme, but Josie said it was best to keep things simple.

That's when I had my brilliant idea. Let's do a life makeover!

'Let's do a what?' Josie asked.

'A life makeover!' I repeated. 'Let's make a checklist of all sorts of stuff about ourselves. Then we can go through it to see what we can change to make us more like Jesus.'

It's normally Josie who comes up with the good ideas. She looked really impressed. I'm not sure but I think tonsillitis may be having quite a positive effect on me.

We spent ages. My life makeover went like this:

1. Be more patient with John even when he's really winding me up.
2. Help Mum more with the housework at the weekends.
3. Try to talk to Jesus every day and not just when I've got a problem I want Him to help me with.
4. Stop worrying about my nose. God made it small and pointy and if He

loves it, I should love it too.

5. Don't get annoyed with Gemma any more, just keep praying for her.

6. Be better about sharing – especially when John wants to borrow my camera.

7. Try to concentrate more in numeracy – it's not Mrs Parker's fault it's boring.

8. Try not to be shy of telling people that I love Jesus.

I think the housework one will be the easiest. Josie says if I keep asking Jesus, He'll help me with all the others too. She said she'd copy her list into her diary when she got home.

And we're going to have 'check-ins' to see how our makeovers are going. Can't wait to tell Louise next Sunday.

Bedtime (Actually I've been in bed for hours, but you know what I mean)

My life makeover's been seriously tested already. John keeps poking his head round my door saying boys' tonsils are fitter than girls' tonsils. That's why he hasn't caught my bugs. I think he's just jealous because he's got to go to school tomorrow and I can stay at home. I told him Josie said her cousin got tonsillitis last year and he's a boy. But he just put his hands over his ears and shouted, 'Not listening!'

Fortunately, Dad came up at that point and told him to leave me alone because I was trying to get better. Unfortunately, Dad then came in to my room with the yellow death juice, but I suppose I can't have everything.

MONDAY 23 NOVEMBER
(Peace at last – John's just gone to school)

Feeling SO much better. I didn't even wake up when Saucy jumped on my bed in the night and stuffed her bottom under my pillow – which is how I found her this morning. And I seem to be able to swallow without feeling as though someone's been at my throat with Dad's electric whizzy round sanding thing. I even managed two Weetabix for breakfast. I think I fancy a doughnut but I'm not sure. Which is fine because we haven't got any anyway.

Just before I got up, I thought I'd work on number 3 on my checklist. So I thanked Jesus that my bugs seemed to be fizzling out. Then I asked Him to look after Josie and help her not feel too tired as it was her first day back at school after the tonsil fever. (She'll have had her last dose of yellow death juice this morning. I won't finish mine until some time on Wednesday … Nice.)

Mum's managed to get another day off work today. She says if I'm still not well tomorrow, she'll have to ask Mrs Allbright to come in.

I said, 'Oh, please, not Mrs Allbright!' She makes you do jigsaw puzzles for hours. If you say, 'Can we do something else now?' her eyes light up and she chuckles, 'I'll just pop next door and pick up some photos for you to look at.' She must have about 199 family photo albums in her house and I'm sure I've already been forced to look through at least 83 of them.

Mum just said I mustn't be unkind. She said Mrs Allbright is a very nice lady who always helps us out when we're in difficulties.

'And anyway,' said Mum, 'now that her husband has died, she'll probably be very glad of your company for the day.'

Talk about missing the point! As if it isn't enough having tonsillitis and being force-fed yellow death juice three times a day. Now I'm expected to keep Mrs Allbright company as well!

I was going to argue that I could look after myself for a few hours, but Mum was wearing one of her 'I'm not going to discuss this any more' expressions. So I thought I'd better leave it for now and have another go later. I suppose if the worst comes to the worst I can always go back to school …

After lunch

Been up all day so far so I'm definitely getting better. Mum's been doing 'pottering' as she calls it. Why is it that whenever grown-ups get five minutes off work, they don't just take the opportunity to slob around reading a book but spend the entire time cleaning? Mum's done all the washing, all the dusting, all the hoovering, she's washed the kitchen floor and she's wiped round in the bathroom. Now she's gone to get on with the ironing. Then this evening she'll be complaining about how tired she is. Is it any wonder?? I did make my bed and fold all the towels neatly in the bathroom (see number 2 on my life makeover list). But she said not to worry and I could help her when I was properly better.

3.00pm

I thought I'd try and do a portrait of Saucy to give
to Mum to say thank you for staying home with me
today. I'd been watching her for ages (Saucy, that
is, not Mum). She'd been lying curled up on the
armchair and hadn't moved. If you didn't know she
was a cat, you'd think she was a cushion.

But the moment I sat down to draw her, guess
what? She opened her eyes, yawned, stretched,
got up, turned round in a circle, plonked down
again and started batting the end of my pencil
with her paws. Then, when she was bored with
that, she turned her back to me, stuck her bottom
in the air, rubbed her head into the cushions and
shoved her tail in my face!

I said, 'Saucy! This is supposed to be a present for my
mum and she won't want a picture of your bottom!' At
which point she flopped down onto the floor,
strolled casually out to the kitchen and started
eating biscuits out of Gruff's bowl. Typical!

So now I'm drawing Mum's orchid instead. It
was a birthday present from Dad and it's had
flowers for over four months now. And it stays
completely still whether you're trying to draw
it or not.

4.30pm

Josie just rang. Unbelievably,
amazingly, incredibly super-duperly,
FANTASMAGORICALLY – she said that, just
before the end of morning break, Gemma went up to
her and asked where I was! If she asked where I was
she must have noticed I'm not there! And if she noticed

I'm not there, maybe she does still like me after all! You don't bother to ask where someone is if you don't care about them, do you?

I said, 'What exactly did she say?'

Josie said, 'She just came over and asked where you were.'

I said, 'But HOW did she ask?'

Josie answered, 'What do you mean, HOW did she ask?'

I said, 'I mean did she ask as if she was really bothered or was she just being nosey?'

Josie thought for a moment then answered, 'Well, it's difficult to tell. But she took the trouble to come over and speak to me which she doesn't normally do. So that must be a good sign.'

I said, 'Do you really think so?'

She said, 'Yes, of course I do. Anyway, I gave her your phone number in case she'd lost it. I told her it would really cheer you up if she rang you for a chat.'

I can't believe it! Gemma's going to ring me for a chat! Everything must be all right again. God's been listening all the time – Gemma hasn't caught tonsillitis and she wants to be friends with me. Thank You, thank You, THANK YOU! Obviously some very positive things come out of praying (and possibly being ill).

5.00pm
Gemma hasn't rung. Maybe she's had to go out.

5.15pm
The phone just went but it was Benny for John. I whispered could he please be quick but he just said, 'Sarah, I'm on the phone,' like Dad does and carried on talking.

5.20pm

They've been on the phone for hours! And it's not as if they're talking about anything important. John's saying something about how much better it'll be when the goalposts are moved because you won't be aiming uphill. I mean, WHO CARES? I'm waiting for a vital phone call which could change the entire course of my life! And they're talking about football!!! Boys are so sad.

5.22pm

Oh, come on, this is ridiculous. Scoring three times in five minutes is just SO not a big deal. WILL YOU GET OFF THE PHONE!!

5.30pm

Mum's just said I've got to leave John alone while he's talking.

I said, 'But, Mum, doesn't he realise I'm waiting for probably the most important phone call of my life?'

She replied totally calmly, 'If it's that important, I'm sure Gemma'll try ringing again if she can't get through.'

I pointed out that none of this would be a problem if I had a mobile. But she said we'd already agreed that John and I could both have mobiles when we started at secondary school.

YOU'VE agreed, you mean. I'D have agreed to have one right now.

5.35pm
Finally! John's off the phone. I expect
Gemma will ring any minute.

5.40pm
Just rang Josie to check she's given
Gemma the right number. She said
she's sure she did.

5.45pm
Oh this is stupid! Why doesn't she just ring?

5.48pm
Perhaps I should ring her.

6.00pm
Mum says supper's ready, and please could I come and
tell her how much I'd like on my plate? I was hungry an
hour ago. Now I just feel sick again.

6.20pm
Back in my room and I'm not coming out until I get
my phone call from Gemma. I managed to eat a little
dollop of mashed potato and about two spoonfuls of
cauliflower cheese. Even that's made my tummy feel
as though it's going to burst. John says it's probably
shrunk over the last few days. He says if I don't start
eating properly soon it'll get smaller and smaller until
it disappears altogether. Then he says I'll have to spend
the rest of my life not being able to eat chocolate
because there'll be nowhere for it to go. I think I prefer
it when he talks about football.
     Now I feel REALLY sick. Got to lie down.

6.35pm

I can't believe it, I can't believe it, I just CAN'T BELIEVE IT! How can one person cause one other person so much MISERY? All Gemma has to do is pick up the phone and say, 'Hi, Sarah. Sorry to hear you're not well. Hope you're back at school really soon.' I mean that honestly is all I'm expecting. It wouldn't even take one whole minute to say. Probably not even half a minute.

Why did Josie have to ring me in the first place? If I didn't know she'd given Gemma my number I wouldn't be expecting anything, would I? I feel like phoning Josie back and saying, 'Thanks so much for ruining a perfectly good Monday.'

But I couldn't do that. Not ever. She's my friend. My best friend. She's worth a million Gemmas. I wish Gemma had never even come to our school. Everything was fine until the wind had to go and blow her in from Scotland. Why can't it just pick her up and blow her back again?

YAY! THERE GOES THE PHONE. MAYBE THIS IS HER.

8.05pm

John's not speaking to me. He says he's never going to bother speaking to me ever again. He's got this box of card tricks that Auntie Jan gave him last Christmas and he said he'd try and take my mind off my lack of phone calls by being clever.

Only I really wasn't in the mood. And because he wouldn't leave me alone, I somehow managed to pick up the whole box of cards and stuff and tip it all out of the window. Dad shouted and Mum said she couldn't believe her eyes. Saucy and Gruff ran for cover, and John said this was the last time he was ever going to bother with me and my shrinking stomach. That was just before he stopped speaking to me.

I don't think Dad's speaking to me either now. He said, 'We've all taken such good care of you while you've been ill and this is the thanks we get.'

Then he went into the kitchen (after he'd been outside and picked up all the cards and stuff).

Bit later
Mum's just been in. Why is it that you can think you've got yourself under total control and you're TOTALLY in the right until someone starts being nice to you? Then all you do is end up looking really pathetic by bursting into floods of tears. Which is exactly what happened when Mum put her arm round me and asked me what the problem was.

I said, 'Why hasn't Gemma rung me? I'm supposed to be her friend. I haven't done a thing to her and now she doesn't even care that I've been in bed ill for days. And I've been praying so hard for her and I really thought God had put it all right, but He hasn't at all.'

'What did Josie actually say?' Mum asked.

I told her.

She smiled (in a wise sort of way, because that's how she usually manages to be in a crisis).

She said, 'Just because Josie gave Gemma your number doesn't mean that Gemma will ring you. And just because Gemma doesn't ring doesn't mean she doesn't care that you're not well. She may be feeling a bit awkward for one thing because she knows she hasn't been very friendly. Maybe she's going to wait until you're back at school and then make it all up with you.'

I sniffed. (I had to, I didn't have a tissue.)

'But what about God?' I said. 'If I've been praying, He should be making it better, shouldn't He?'

Mum gave me a big squeeze and said, 'You can't hurry God. He does things in His own time, not in ours. You've just got to keep talking to Him. Whatever He's doing, it'll be for the best. I know it's hard when you want something so much, but you have to learn to be patient.'

She's said that before. About being patient. Don't think I'm very good at it.

Then Mum said I'm still not well and need at least another day at home. She's fixed it for Mrs Allbright to come in. Haven't got the energy to argue.

Bedtime
Just had a huge hug with John and Dad.

I said to John, 'I'm really sorry about your cards. You were being nice and I was horrible.'

John said, 'That's all right, I'm used to it.'

So I hit him with the box of tissues Mum had just given me.

Then Dad said we must both get to bed, especially me because I was looking pale and tired – except for my eyes, John said. He told me they were all red and disgusting. I hit him with the tissues again.

Got such a headache, but I've got to write this down.

Dear Lord God,
Thank You that You never go away.
Sometimes it feels as though You're not
there, but You are. Always. I'm sorry I got
angry with Gemma today, and that I even felt
cross with Josie. And I'm sorry I was so mean
to John. It's not his fault about Gemma.

Please help me to be patient. I can't do it
on my own. I just end up getting annoyed
with everybody. I know You love me and I
know You love Gemma too. Help us to be
friends again soon – and help Gemma to
know that You're her friend for ever.

I feel better now I've said sorry.

TUESDAY, 24 NOVEMBER

8.30-ish am (Just realised it's only a month till Christmas Eve!!!)

Just had breakfast with Mum. She says Mrs Allbright
will be in, in about half an hour.

I said, 'Mum, couldn't I just come to work with you?
I'd be really quiet.'

Mum said. 'No, you'll be much better off at home.
Anyway, Mrs Allbright's looking forward to it.'

'Well, I'm not,' I mumbled. Mum heard.

She said, 'Sarah, my love, what were you so upset
about yesterday?'

I frowned. Was this a trick question?

'Gemma not being my friend,' I answered slowly.

'Exactly,' said Mum. 'Well, Mrs Allbright needs friends too. Think how upset she'd be if she thought you didn't want to spend a bit of time with her.'

A BIT of time? We're talking about all day here!

I said I bet Mrs Allbright had lots of friends. Mum said that didn't mean she wouldn't like to have me as a friend too – which seemed like a good moment to point out that she is at least 159 years older than me. What on earth would we have to talk about? But Mum just put her hand on mine and shook her head.

'You'll think of something,' she said. 'Anyway, she's not <u>that</u> old.'

I said, 'But she treats me like a baby.'

Mum said, 'Well, you'd better show her you aren't one then, hadn't you?'

Then she looked at the clock and said, 'Oh my goodness, is that the time?' and went bustling off. (She bustled back almost immediately and said she was very sorry but she'd have to have her watch back. She said she'd try and remember to get some batteries for my clock while she was out.)

Perhaps it'll be better not knowing the time so much today. At least I won't be able to see how slowly it's dragging.

There goes the doorbell. Must be Mrs Allbright. Maybe I can get away with just staying up here in my room all day. Great, now Mum's calling me down. There's no escape. Whoop-de-doo.

Evening

For a day that looked as if it was going to be REALLY bad, it actually turned out to be not that bad after all. Mrs Allbright arrived with practically a suitcase full of jigsaw puzzles. I thought my teeth would fall out with boredom. But when I asked (very politely), 'Would you mind if we didn't do jigsaw puzzles today?' she said, of course not. I was the one who wasn't well and I must feel free to do exactly what I wanted.

So we watched a bit of TV together (a daytime talky programme about what your curtains say about you – mmm) and then she asked if I wanted a drink. I said could I please have some hot chocolate. She asked if I'd like it with real chocolate grated on the top because she just happened to have a big bar in her bag. So of course I said, yes please. (I mean, it would have been rude to say no.)

After that, Mrs Allbright suggested playing Cluedo (which she also happened to have in her bag). I was amazed because she doesn't look like the Cluedo-playing sort. She said that her husband used to hate playing games. But for some reason he loved jigsaw puzzles and Cluedo (she said he fancied himself as a bit of a detective), and they used to play it for hours.

Then she said, 'This is a real treat for me. I haven't had this game out of its box since he died.'

I wasn't sure what to say. So I asked, 'Do you miss him?'

'Oh yes,' she smiled (sadly, I thought), 'every single day.'

I was a bit worried that she might dig into her bag again and bring out at least 197 photos of him for me to look through, but she didn't. She never even <u>mentioned</u> photographs, and when Mum got home I felt a bit guilty about the jigsaw puzzles. So I said I was sorry we hadn't done any.

Can you believe it, but she said, 'Don't you go worrying about that, dear. To be honest, I find jigsaws rather boring.'

Then, just as she was leaving, Josie appeared. Mum had offered Mrs Allbright a cup of tea but she'd said she wouldn't stop any longer. She said her goldfish were probably beginning to think she'd left home. I said I didn't realise goldfish noticed things like that. Mrs Allbright winked at me and said, 'If you ask me, goldfish notice a lot more than people give them credit for.'

That got me thinking about spiders and ants and all sorts of other creepy-crawly things that we think of as a bit brainless, and tend to stamp on a lot (rather unkindly really) just for being creepy and crawly (and wiggly).

I said to Josie, 'I wonder whether they notice when a massive great boot comes hurtling down at them? Do you suppose they nearly always get squished because they just don't see it coming? Or DO they see it coming but can't get out of the way quick enough?'

Josie said it wasn't something she'd ever really thought about. I said well, she ought to. After all, creepy things had been made by God just as much as non-creepy things like ostriches and people. So I guessed He loved them too and didn't want to see them squished onto the bottom of someone's boot.

Then I made a decision never to stamp on anything creepy or crawly or wiggly ever again and to try to stop other people from doing it too.

'I could start an anti-squishing campaign,' I said. 'I could call it something like … "Let The Creepers Crawl".'

At which point I noticed that Josie was looking at me rather oddly.

'What's wrong?' I asked.

She said there was nothing wrong with her. But she was beginning to wonder if my tonsillitis had affected my brain because I didn't usually waffle on this much.

I said, 'Really? I thought I did,' and then I said, 'Aren't people full of surprises?'

Josie asked (looking at me even more oddly), 'What people?'

'Just people,' I said, 'but especially Mrs Allbright.'

I told her that when Mrs Allbright had arrived, I thought she was going to bore me to a heap, but in the end we'd had a surprisingly good day. I said I might go and visit her sometimes (especially as it turned out I wouldn't have to do jigsaw puzzles), because she only had her goldfish for company. And I thought old people didn't deserve to be lonely like that.

Then I asked Josie if she'd come round for a special reason and for a moment she couldn't remember. She did in the end, though. She'd brought a letter over from school about the end of term school trip. We're going to a 'living' museum, where you can walk through a Victorian street and look in shop windows

at real displays of old things. There are pretend shopkeepers and customers and policemen around dressed in old-fashioned clothes.

Josie thought it sounded really interesting. I asked if I could sit next to her on the coach.

She said, yes, of course, but Gemma might want to sit next to me by that time.

I said, 'Not a chance. I've been <u>dying</u> here for the last five days and she hasn't even bothered to ring me up.'

'I know,' Josie replied.

'<u>How</u> do you know?' I said.

'Because I asked her today if she'd rung you,' Josie answered.

'And what did she say?' I asked.

'She said "no",' Josie said, and gave me one of her looks.

I couldn't think of anything else to ask then so I just went, 'Oh,' and tried not to look disappointed.

Josie said she had to go but I wasn't to give up on Gemma. After all, if I thought Mrs Allbright was full of surprises, imagine how much more full of surprises God must be.

'I mean,' she said, 'think about it. He's so huge and so powerful and He loves us so much.' Then she said, 'Just because the Gemma thing's not sorted out yet, you mustn't give up praying about it. Sometimes I think we're supposed to do that. You know, keep on praying even when nothing seems to change, because then God will see how much we really want something.'

Fab! Supper's ready. I'm starving this evening.

Bedtime

Mum says I can go back to school tomorrow. She says I've eaten so much pasta bake I must be feeling better. John added (quite kindly for him) that I needn't worry about my tummy disappearing any more because it's obviously re-stretched itself.

I'm going to pray about the Gemma thing again. But there's something almost more important I need to say tonight (which surprises me a bit). I want to tell God I'm sorry for being mean about Mrs Allbright this morning. She's really an amazing person. She's made me see that it doesn't matter if we're young people or old people – we can all get on together and we're all special to God because He made us.

(Mum's just been in with batteries for my clock. She says she doesn't want to give me any excuses for getting up late in the morning.)

Josie's right, God is full of surprises. I think I made a new friend today.

WEDNESDAY, 25 NOVEMBER
8.15am

YAY! Just had my last spoonful of Dr F-W's yellow death juice! If I ever get tonsillitis again I shall refuse all medication that's yellow and doesn't at least taste of strawberries or chocolate. Got to go. I didn't get up late, it just seemed to take about three times longer than normal to do everything. Maybe that's what happens after you've been ill – you fall into a kind of slow-motion mode without realising it until it's too late and you're about to miss your bus.

After school

So, the big question is ARE THEY OR AREN'T THEY?

I walked into the cloakroom this morning and loads of people said, 'Oh, hi, are you better?' I nearly said, 'No, I'm still really ill, but I thought if I came back to school you'd all get the chance of catching it.' (Didn't, though.) Then Gemma walked in. I saw her look at me so I smiled. She didn't smile back but she didn't exactly blank me either, which I thought must be vaguely positive.

Ten minutes later, Mrs Parker was doing the register. She said it was nice to see me back and carried on ticking down the list. But when she called out Gemma's name, there was no answer. I looked round and her place was empty.

'No Gemma today?' Mrs Parker asked.

I was about to say, yes, I'd just seen her in the cloakroom when Charlotte Miller said, 'She's crying in the toilets, Miss.'

I thought Mrs Parker looked a bit annoyed, which she shouldn't have done because if anyone's crying it means they're upset. They need someone to be kind to them, not annoyed with them. I'm sure I heard her mutter, 'Oh, not again.' But out loud she said, 'Charlotte, will you go and fetch her, please?'

Charlotte shook her head and said, 'She won't come with me. I've already tried.'

This could be it, I thought, this could be my moment to put everything right. So I shot my hand straight up and said, 'I'll go, Miss.'

Mrs Parker sighed and said, 'Tell her I want to see her immediately. She's late for registration.' (I thought that was a bit mean because maybe what Gemma needed more than anything was someone to chat to.)

As it turned out, I didn't get as far as the toilets. Gemma was already on her way to class when I saw her, so there wasn't the opportunity to talk about anything. Also she just sort of brushed past me and her eyes were really red. Mrs Parker didn't tell her off.

At morning break there was no sign of Gemma anywhere. I checked every single toilet cubicle and I got John to check in the boys' (well, you never know). Nothing. So I said to Josie, 'You don't think she's run away, do you?'

Josie said she was sure she hadn't. But if she wasn't in class after break, perhaps we ought to point it out to Mrs Parker. I said wouldn't Mrs Parker notice anyway? But Josie said that teachers can sometimes get a bit stressy which makes them more likely to miss things. Like that time in science last year when Stephen Small managed to get from the front of the classroom all the way to the back without being seen. He did it by wriggling along the floor between everyone's feet underneath the tables. He'd probably have got away with it completely, AND had time to wriggle all the way back again, if Charlotte Miller hadn't dropped her pencil case on his head. That made him say 'Ow!' really loudly. (Later Charlotte said she'd dropped the pencil case by accident, but Stephen Small didn't believe her.) Anyway, that was the end of his morning breaks for the rest of the term. (He's moved to Wales now. Even Mum said Wales was welcome to him.)

Then I remembered it was Charlotte Miller who'd said Gemma was crying in the toilets. I suddenly thought, if she's not bothered about dropping pencil cases on people's heads, perhaps it was her who'd upset Gemma and made her end up crying in the toilets in the first place.

Josie said, 'You can't jump to conclusions about people like that!'

I said, 'I know. All I'm going to do is ask Charlotte if she knows why Gemma keeps disappearing, and that might be enough to get her to confess.'

'Confess what?' Josie asked.

'Whether or not she upset Gemma in the toilets this morning, of course!' I said (a bit snappily because my patience was 'wearing mighty thin' as Dad says). So to make it better I added, 'PLEASE come with me, Josie. I really want you to.'

Josie didn't look as if she thought this was a very good plan. But I felt this whole Gemma thing had been going on for far too long and it was about time someone got to the bottom of it. And I was beginning to feel (because of the crying in the toilets which couldn't possibly have had anything to do with me) that perhaps Gemma falling out with me wasn't my fault after all.

But it's weird. In this school, whole children can just disappear into thin air during morning break and then reappear again in time for science! And no one has the faintest clue where they've been! We still had five minutes till the bell went, but could we find Charlotte? Could we bananas!

Josie said perhaps God didn't mean us to find her because He didn't want us to go poking our noses in. So I said, 'What about the times when Louise says God wants us to stop messing around and just get on and do the right thing? This could be one of those times.'

Josie wasn't sure that that meant trying to get confessions out of people (she remembered later that Louise had been talking about being prepared to give up our time to help someone in need). But she said she'd talk to Charlotte at lunchtime with me anyway.

Lunchtime seemed ages away – especially as, when she reappeared from wherever she'd been hiding, Gemma had red eyes again. And Charlotte Miller was definitely giggling about something.

So, about a million years later, there we were ready to get in the lunch queue when I saw Charlotte going into the cloakroom.

I nudged Josie and said, 'There she is!'

Josie said excitedly, 'I think I can smell chocolate pudding.'

I said, 'If we catch her now, she'll be more or less on her own.'

Josie said, 'Where there's a smell of chocolate pudding, there usually IS chocolate pudding.'

I sighed. 'Josie, some things are more important than food.'

She gave me one of those 'yeah, right' looks, but came with me anyway. Which I suppose was really good of her because we only have chocolate pudding about twice a term.

I pushed open the cloakroom door. Charlotte was on her own by her peg, fiddling about in her bag.

This was it.

I said pointedly to Josie, 'Mmm, no sign of Gemma in here.' Then I said (quite cleverly I thought), 'But Charlotte's over there, maybe she'll know where she is.'

Charlotte glanced round.

'What?'

'Have you seen Gemma?' I asked.

'Why should I have seen her?' Charlotte answered.

'Oh, I don't know.' I shrugged. Then I added, casually, 'By the way, did you find out what was wrong with her this morning?'

Charlotte flicked her eyes from me to Josie and back again. I felt my heart start beating faster. I'd done it. I'd cracked her! Any moment now, a confession would come pouring from her lips!

Then –

'What are you girls doing in here? You should be lining up for lunch.'

It was Mrs Parker and she didn't look happy.

Josie said, 'Sorry, Miss, we were just about to.'

'Well, off you go then,' Mrs Parker snapped.

NO! Just a few more minutes, that's all I needed. I looked at Josie desperately. She looked back at me as if to say, 'Oh well, think of it this way. At least we still get to have chocolate pudding.'

Mrs Parker stood sternly holding open the cloakroom door. We all shuffled through. I couldn't believe it. She'd ruined everything. Didn't she realise I was on the point of uncovering the grisly truth? Teachers just have no respect for what goes on behind the closed door of a cloakroom.

The lunch queue had gone down quite a bit. But Charlotte still managed to push in by standing next to one of her friends and pretending she'd been saving her a place.

That was it. I couldn't wait any longer. So, without saying a word to Josie, I stepped out of the queue and marched straight up to her.

'Charlotte,' I said, wondering if this was possibly the stupidest thing I'd ever done in my life (I'd remembered that Charlotte's cousin is one of the Dixons Gang and they hate all us Topz), 'I'm sorry to ask, but was it you who upset Gemma this morning?'

For a moment she just looked at me. Then she glanced at her friend. Then they both burst out laughing. Everyone was looking at me now. This was NOT a good way to feel.

When she'd stopped laughing Charlotte said, 'Sarah, I'm sorry to tell you that if Gemma wants to spend all her time crying in the toilets, it's got nothing to do with me. It's not MY fault her parents are splitting up and she's moving back to Scotland.'

Josie said I gaped. You know, just stared at Charlotte with my mouth open – a bit like a photo of a big-mouthed fish.

In fact I felt a bit like a photo of a big-mouthed fish.

I couldn't move. I just stood there … gaping.

7.30pm

Josie phoned me. She said she'd been thinking. She said, as most people may not know about Gemma's parents breaking up, we shouldn't spread it around. She said Gemma was obviously really upset at the moment and wouldn't want people talking about her. Anyway, it wasn't kind to gossip. I said even if it was true – which we don't actually know for definite because Gemma hardly talks to Josie and hasn't spoken to me for ages – I had no intention of spreading it around.

BIG mistake. John happened to be walking past me on his way to the kitchen at that very moment (only to get a bowl of cornflakes, he said later, but I think he was spying). So he stopped and said, 'Spreading what around?'

I turned my back on him but he came and stood right behind me and put his chin on my shoulder.

'Spreading what around?' he repeated.

I shrugged him off and said didn't he know it was extremely rude to listen to other people's private phone calls? But he wouldn't go away. I had to tell Josie I'd ring her back later when my nosey brother wasn't earwigging, and went off into my bedroom.

Mum came in and asked me why I slammed the door.

I said, 'I didn't. I just closed it firmly.' Then I said, in a very grown-up voice, 'Isn't it possible to have any privacy in this house?'

7.40pm

Just been in to Mum to say sorry. It's not her fault John's a nerd. I suppose.

8.00pm

Yes, 8 o'clock, that's all it is and Mum's saying I need to think about getting ready for bed.

I said, 'But, Mum, it's only 8 o'clock.'

She said, 'Exactly, and you've had a long day at school having just got over tonsillitis. You need sleep.'

I said, 'What I really need is to speak to Josie.'

Mum said, 'You've just BEEN speaking to her.'

I said, 'I know, but John was listening so we couldn't talk properly. Please. It's very important. Can't I just give her a really quick call?'

Mum said, 'If there's one thing you and Josie never have it's a really quick call. Whatever it is, I'm sure it can wait until you see her at school tomorrow.'

I said, 'But supposing I don't see her tomorrow? Supposing something happens in the night like a huge earthquake? What if our house gets swallowed up into a big black hole? And what if we have to live the

rest of our lives in an underground
city surrounded by strange green
Martians who've been transported
there through space from another
planet?'

Mum had already left the room and shut
the door behind her by then, though, so she didn't
hear me. Which is probably a good thing.

8.15pm (Nearly anyway)
I SO need a mobile. Perhaps I could
save up for one. I could get a job in a
chip shop. Oh no I couldn't. Not old
enough. Awwww!

8.20pm
Poo to John. Why does he have to have such a big nose
anyway?

In bed
When I was on the phone to Josie, she said (about the
trying to get Charlotte to confess thing) that she never
knew I could be like that.

I said, 'Like what? Secret agenty?'

She said, 'No. Sneaky.'

Still in bed
Perhaps that's something I should pray about.

Still still in bed
What is wrong with me? Gemma might be facing a
really massive crisis and I haven't even prayed for her
this evening! Here I am supposed to be giving my life a

makeover and I haven't bothered to pray for someone with a huge problem. I think it must be the shock. I hope it's the shock. I mean I just can't believe that Gemma's had all this going on without telling me when we were supposed to be friends.

Perhaps I'm just a really selfish person.

I don't believe it. There I go again, thinking about myself instead of about Gemma. Just quit yabbing, Sarah, and pray. NOW.

THURSDAY, 26 NOVEMBER
(Just woken up)
I've just noticed that my diary entries seem to be getting longer and longer. Perhaps that's what happens – the more you write, the more you <u>want</u> to write. Or is it that when you start writing about it, your life seems to become that much more interesting and so there's just endless stuff to say? Must ask Louise.

Mum's calling. That's the funny thing about parents. They nag you to go to bed, then as soon as it's morning, they're nagging you to get up again.

Why can't they make up their minds?

After breakfast
Have a horrible feeling I may have fallen asleep praying last night. I wonder if Jesus gets that a lot – people dozing off in the middle of what they're saying to Him? Hope He knows it's not that my prayer wasn't important. It's just that I was really tired.

I'd better tell Him later.

No, I'll tell Him now.

8.15am

Glad I've cleared that up.

Hope Josie's on the bus. We really need to talk.

4.45pm

Josie's just gone home. I wanted her to stay for supper but she has a piano lesson.

I feel SO bad. Not only does Gemma now think I've been gossiping behind her back (which I haven't), she also thinks I've been spreading rumours around school about her parents splitting up (which I honestly wouldn't). I didn't even hear about it until yesterday and I still don't know if it's true.

Josie wasn't on the bus so we didn't have a chance to talk properly till morning break. And even then it was really difficult because it's been raining all day. So we couldn't go outside and find somewhere private.

Josie said we could get out a board game in the classroom and look as if we were playing. That way no one would notice we were really having a serious conversation. Only, after about three seconds, John and Dave came over and asked if they could play as well, so we had to give up that idea.

There were girls hanging around in the cloakroom. Mrs Francis was putting up an Egyptian display in the hall and the Year 4s were playing hide and seek in the toilets. I'm telling you, school is a zoo.

Finally we tried to grab five minutes in the library. We hovered in the corner in the science section (next to the 'G/H' shelves), and when anyone came near, pulled a book out and said things like 'Mmm, have you read this one?' and 'This is an interesting cover.'

Josie whispered, 'I think we should just try and

forget what Charlotte said.'

'And how are we supposed to do that?' I asked.

Josie said, 'I don't know. Let's <u>pretend</u> to forget it then.'

I said, 'But supposing Gemma's desperate for someone to talk to. How can I help her if I pretend I don't know what's going on?'

'But that's the whole point,' Josie said. 'We DON'T know what's going on. It could just be Charlotte stirring.'

'I suppose,' I said. 'It all makes sense, though. It explains why Gemma's been so upset.'

Josie said, 'Mmm, have you read this one?' She grabbed a book with a picture of a man on the front holding an apple in one hand and a feather pen in the other.

Mrs Ellis was about to walk by with a clipboard under her arm.

'All right, girls?' she asked, which is teacher-speak for, 'I'm just passing through and haven't got time for a conversation but felt I ought to say something.'

'Yes, Miss,' we said and she disappeared round the corner.

'The thing is,' Josie went on, 'if Gemma <u>was</u> desperate for someone to talk to, I'm sure she would have told you everything by now. After all, you were her first friend here. If she was going to tell anyone, it would have been you.'

I said, 'Which is exactly the bit I can't understand. If MY parents were breaking up, I'd be talking to you about it all the time.'

That was the moment my day turned into a disgusting, oozing pit of slime.

Charlotte Miller suddenly stepped out from behind the geography section. She had a really evil grin on her face.

She said, 'There you are, Gemma. I told you they were in here gossiping. You see, it's not me who's been spreading rumours at all.'

I looked at Gemma.

I wanted to die. Well, not die exactly, but I wished the earthquake thing had actually happened in the night. I'd rather have been spending the rest of my life looking at ugly Martians than standing in the library looking at Gemma – who was staring at me as if she hated every bone in my body.

5.45pm (Dad's home)
Just popped downstairs for some lemonade. The lid wasn't on properly so all the fizz has gone.

Dad came into the kitchen and said, 'Are you all right, poppet? You look a bit pale.'

I said, 'Yes, I'm fine. Do you mind if I go back upstairs?'

He said, 'You're sure you're all right, though?'

I said, 'Yes, really. Do you mind if I go back upstairs?'

He said, 'Well … as long as there's nothing wrong.'

I said, 'There's nothing wrong. I'm just going back upstairs.'

He opened his mouth to say something else. I had the feeling that this could go on all evening so I said, 'I really need the loo,' and shot off before he could ask if I was all right again.

If only he knew. I'm not all right. I don't think I'm ever going to be all right again. At the very least I'm going to have to try and get him and Mum to let me change schools.

The absolute worst part of the library thing was that Charlotte said, 'I thought you two were all churchy. You're not supposed to be into talking about people behind their backs. I can't imagine God being very pleased.'

Gemma looked from me to Josie and back to me. Then she stomped off.

Next time we saw her, her eyes were all red again. So was her nose.

Charlotte was smirking.

I said to Josie, 'We've got to tell her we weren't talking about her.'

Josie said, 'We can't.'

I said, 'Why not?'

She said, 'Because we were talking about her.'

I said, 'But we weren't being nasty!'

'It doesn't matter,' she said. 'We were still sticking our noses in. At least, that's the way Gemma will see it.'

Gemma spoke to me after lunch.

She came right up to me and said, 'You're the meanest person I've ever known.'

I want to tell Mum but I can't. I didn't mean to but I've ruined everything and let everyone down – Gemma, Josie (I should never have dragged her into it in the first place). And God.

And I'm sorry, Louise, but writing it down doesn't help one bit.

8.30pm

Mum just came in to say goodnight.

She said, 'Is everything all right?'

I said, 'Yeah.'

She said, 'Nothing's happened with Josie, has it?'

I said, 'No, of course not.'

She said, 'All right. Let me know if there's anything you want.'

I want a cuddle.

FRIDAY, 27 NOVEMBER

5.30am

What am I going to do? I feel so guilty. I can't even talk to Mum and I can always talk to Mum about everything.

5.40am

I've just spent the last five minutes sucking on the back of my tongue to see if I can make my tonsils all big and uncomfortable again so I don't have to go to school.

Don't think it's worked.

Ow. Now I've got a really sore tongue.

6.00am

Perfect. Even Saucy doesn't want to know me. She's flounced off because I was trying to cuddle her. When I think of the hours I've put up with her NITS!

6.05am

If I had a mobile I could ring Josie and see if she's awake. I suppose if she wasn't she wouldn't be very pleased, though.

6.25am

Had to go and get a drink of milk. Dad came down just after me. He was all dressed and everything. He asked what I was doing up so early. I said I was thirsty. Then he put his arm round me. He said he had to go to work in a minute but he had time for a quick chat if I wanted one.

I said, 'No, that's all right.'

Just as he was going out of the front door he said, 'Your mum's awake if you want to go in and see her.'

6.30am

I do want to go in and see her. I just can't.

8.15am

Had breakfast with Mum.
  She said, 'You're quiet.'
  I said, 'Yes.'

After school

Horrible, horrible, HORRIBLE day.

  I whispered to Josie on the bus this morning that I was going to try to explain things to Gemma. I said I had to. I couldn't stick going through another day with her thinking I'm the biggest creep on the planet.

  But sorting things out never happened. Gemma wasn't at school.

  Even Mrs Parker was off sick. We had this supply teacher who got really flustered every time someone asked her a question.

  AND she kept calling me Sophie. I must have told her a million times my name's Sarah but it didn't make the slightest bit of difference. So in the end I thought, what's the point? I may as well just answer to Sophie!

  Now everyone's calling me Sophie. Even John. And he's not even in my class.

5.50pm

Dad's just taken John to youth club.

  After supper, Mum had said to go and get ready otherwise we'd be late.

  I'd said, 'I'm not going.'
  She'd asked, 'Why?'
  I'd said, 'I just don't feel like it today.'

She'd said, 'Is Josie going?'

I'd answered, 'I don't know.'

She'd asked, 'What is it? Are you still not feeling well?'

I'd said, 'I feel fine, I just don't want to go to youth club.'

So John had grabbed his coat and said, 'Fair enough. See you later, Sophie.'

7.30pm

Do you suppose all mums are perfect or is it just mine?

After John went, she brought me up a massive bowl of chocolate orange ice cream and sat on the rug with me in my room. She said she thought I could do with cheering up. I said I was all right, really I was.

She said, 'Well, something's rattling your cage.'

I didn't answer for a moment. I had this funny picture in my head of me sitting in a giant rabbit hutch. Gemma was sprawled across the roof, rocking the whole thing backwards and forwards madly with all her teeth showing.

Then Mum said, 'What's wrong, Sarah?' And that's when the bursting into tears thing happened again. Bursting into tears is really annoying any old time. But when you've got a mouthful of chocolate orange ice cream, it's worse than annoying because everything gets all gooey and slurpy. I couldn't swallow and I didn't want to spit it out. I could feel it all beginning to dribble down my chin. I must have looked like a puffy, red-eyed monster with a brown beard.

Mum didn't say anything, though. She just took the bowl of ice cream from me and gave me a tissue.

Then I told her everything.

She said, 'Sarah, my love, why didn't you tell me yesterday?'

I said I couldn't. I mean, what if she thought I was horrible too?

Mum said, 'Nothing you do will ever make me think you're horrible. And anyway, what is it you've done that's so bad? Nothing. What's happened is that Charlotte's tried to cause trouble and done a good job. As far as Gemma's concerned, this is just a huge misunderstanding. And misunderstandings can be sorted out.'

'But Charlotte said God wouldn't be pleased with us,' I said, a bit sobbily (quite a lot sobbily, actually). 'How can anything get sorted out if God's angry with me?'

Mum said, 'When we do something wrong, it doesn't make God angry. It makes Him sad. He knows that doing the wrong thing not only makes other people unhappy, it can make us unhappy too. And God loves us so much, He wants what's best for us so that we can be happy. So if you think you've done something wrong, then you must say sorry to Him. As soon as you've said sorry and you mean it, He'll forgive you. You'll know that everything's all right between you again and God isn't sad any more.'

I didn't say anything straight away. I needed to think about all of that.

Mum went on, 'But if you've told me everything exactly as it happened, then I'm sure you don't have anything to say sorry for. You were only trying to find a way to help. God knows that. And God knows you. He knows you inside out and back to front. He knows what you think. He knows what you're going to say before you say it, and what you're going to do before you do it. He knows how much you care about Gemma. You've been praying for her for days and He's been listening to you.'

'Fee fasn't, fough,' I spluttered. (I'd just shovelled in some more ice cream and it had gone so melty and mushy I'm surprised I even got that much out.)

I noticed that Mum was looking at me sort of blankly.

I waited until my mouth was empty (so did she) and repeated, 'He hasn't, though. If He'd really been listening to me, things could never have ended up as bad as this.'

She said, 'Nothing's "ended up" like anything. I told you before, you have to be patient. God does things when He's ready, not when we want Him to. He waits for the best time. I mean, who knows? Maybe this has all happened because God wants to show you that there's someone else in your class who needs praying for at the moment besides Gemma.'

I thought for a minute but as no one popped into my head straight away I asked, 'Who?'

'Charlotte,' Mum said.

'But Mum!' I wailed. 'Charlotte practically HATES me!'

'Exactly,' Mum said, 'and if there's one thing God hates, it's hatred.'

8.45pm

Just been to say goodnight to Dad.

He said, 'You're looking better.'

I said, 'Yes. I'm <u>feeling</u> better.'

I haven't been mean to Gemma, but I've told God I'm sorry for listening to stuff about her. It's wrong to listen to gossip. Unless she tells me herself that her parents have split up, that's what it is, isn't it – that stuff Charlotte said? GOSSIP!

I asked Mum if there was anything I could do to say sorry to Gemma too. Trouble is, she thinks I'm the meanest person she's ever known and she'd probably rather have a conversation with an earwig. Mum said why didn't I try writing her a letter? She said even if I decided not to give it to her in the end, it would still help me. At least I'd be able to say sorry in the way I want to say it. So I think I'll do that tomorrow.

Haven't prayed for Charlotte yet. I'm not sure what to say. Perhaps I'll do that tomorrow too.

John came in to tell me youth club was brilliant and I'd missed doughnuts.

I said, 'Thanks.'

He said, 'You're welcome. See you in the morning, Sophie.'

(Sigh.)

SATURDAY, 28 NOVEMBER
After breakfast

Although he drives me nuts most
of the time, sometimes I quite like
having a brother.

I went downstairs to have
breakfast and he shoved a plastic
lunch box at me and said, 'Don't say I
never give you anything.'

Inside were two doughnuts.

I said, 'Wow. Thanks, John.'

John said, 'Well, you were looking so ugly last
night I thought you could do with a treat.'

I gave him a shove. His elbow went in his bowl of Rice
Krispies. They tipped out and the milk went all over the
table. At which point Mum came in.

'Who's been making all this mess?' she said.

'Nothing to do with me,' I said innocently. 'I've got
doughnuts.'

Then Dad put his head round the door and asked,
'Anyone for a walk in the park with Gruff?'

I said, 'No thanks, not this morning. I've got to write
a letter. John wants to go, though. He can dry out his
soaking wet elbow in the breeze.'

John threw his spoon at me. I dodged so it missed
completely and went flying across the kitchen. So far,
today is going REALLY well.

10.45am

Josie just rang to say her dad's taking her ice skating
this afternoon and would I like to come? Brilliant!
They're picking me up at half past one. I've only been
once before with all the rest of the Topz Gang when

Benny invited us for his birthday. I was useless but it was SO fun.

I said to Josie maybe she could help me write this sorry letter to Gemma. I've been trying for ages but I don't seem to know how to start.

She said, 'What have you got so far?'

I said, 'Dear Gemma.'

Hang on. Something's happened. I can hear John storming about downstairs. Back soon.

Oh no. GRUFF'S GONE.

4.00pm

I can't believe it. He really has gone. We've looked everywhere. I've been calling 'Gruff!' so much I feel as if I've got tonsillitis again. There's just no sign of him.

It turns out that John and Dad were down the bottom end of the park with him, near the pond. John saw Danny and Dave playing football and went to join in for a few minutes. Suddenly he heard Dad shouting and when he looked over, Dad was tearing across the grass towards the trees. John says he'd never seen him move so fast so he knew something was wrong.

All three of them shot after him. When they finally caught him up, Dad was so out of breath he could hardly speak. But between all the huffing and puffing, John managed to work out that Gruff had taken off after a cat and disappeared into the trees.

John said they called and called. Either Gruff didn't hear or he was still too busy chasing the cat to notice, because he never came back. Dad reckoned they should split up because they could cover twice as much ground that way. So he went in one direction and John and Danny went in another. Dave said he'd wait near the pond in case Gruff suddenly showed up back there again. But nothing.

I can't understand it. I mean, sometimes Gruff does chase off after cats but he always gives up really quickly and comes right back. Why he goes after them in the first place is just weird anyway. Doesn't he realise he lives with a cat? Errr … no, I don't think he does. I've always had this sneaky suspicion he thinks Saucy's a dog – which I suppose isn't all that surprising because she does spend half her time playing with his toys and eating out of his bowl. (For some reason, Gruff never goes near hers though. Perhaps it's the smell. Cat food – bleaah.)

Josie and her dad joined in looking for Gruff. They turned up to go ice skating, but when Mum told them what had happened, Josie said she'd stay and help find Gruff instead.

I said, 'Josie, you really don't have to.'

She said, 'Don't be silly. Anyway, skating won't be nearly so much fun without you there to laugh at.'

Mum didn't come with us. Our phone number's on a disk on Gruff's collar and she wanted to be here in case anyone rang saying they'd found him. No one has, though.

Everyone's gone home now. Dad's just having a cup of tea. Then he says we'll have one more hunt. If there's still no sign, perhaps we should call in at the police station. John's gone to find a photo of him to hand in – Gruff, that is, not Dad. He says maybe we could put up some posters.

4.20pm

Dad's STILL drinking tea. I wish he'd hurry up. John and I finished our juice ages ago.

I thought the last couple of days had been bad but this is AWFUL. Poor Gruff, he could be anywhere. He might be all wet and cold and shivery and lost in a car park or something without a clue how to find his way home.

I said to Dad, 'How can you spend ages and AGES drinking tea when Gruff's out there all on his own? Something terrible might have happened to him.'

Then I thought of the absolute worst thing of all. Supposing someone had spotted him and kidnapped him! I mean he is the most adorable-looking, scrawny old scruff bag. And he's so friendly with everyone (except if you're a cat). If I saw him out on his own, <u>I'd</u> want to take him home. I was going to say something but John was looking so upset already I thought it would only make things worse.

Mum said, 'Let Dad finish his tea. Then we'll all go out and have another look.'

I whispered, 'But Mum, what if we never see him again?'

She whispered back, 'Of course we'll see him again. Go and ask God to take care of him till we find him. He's good at things like that.'

So that's what I'm doing. Asking. Over and over and OVER again.

Dad's calling. Time to go.

7.30pm

We've searched and searched and searched. We've been everywhere. He's gone for ever, I know it. John's crying in his room. He never cries. I want to cry but I can't. I just keep seeing Gruff's little face in my head. His eyes are so sad. I can hear him whimpering, 'What are you doing? Why have you stopped looking for me?'

We went to the police station but nobody had taken him in. The policeman at the desk was really kind though. I told him that even though Gruff's name is Gruff, that's not what he's like at all and he's just a big old softie. Then John showed him the photo and he even rang the local dog warden for us to see if a dog like Gruff had been picked up today. But, no, it hadn't.

Dad said it was too dark to keep on looking.

Mum made pizza but nobody wanted any.

7.50pm

Phone just rang.

Dad got there first.

It was Josie.

She said, 'Hi. Have you found him?'

I said, 'No. We thought you might be someone ringing to say you'd got him.'

She said, 'Oh, sorry. Mum said I shouldn't phone and I should wait till I heard from you. But I just wanted to know.'

I said, 'Don't worry about it.'

She said, 'Mum says would you like to come here for a sleepover tonight to take your mind off things.'

I said that was a really nice thought, but nothing would take my mind off things. Anyway, I wanted to be here in case Gruff suddenly turned up.

Josie said that was fine and she'd feel the same. She said she'd just keep praying that he'd be all right and we'd find him.

I said, 'Thanks, so will I.'

One thing's for sure. Whatever else happens, it can never be as bad as this.

8.00pm

Went in to see John. He'd got all his photos of Gruff out on the bed, right from when he was a tiny puppy. There's a really cute one where he's nosing inside Mum's peg bag when it fell off the washing line. All you can see is his back half and his stumpy little tail stuck up in the air.

John looks so miserable.

I said, 'He's got to come back. He's just got to.'

John said, 'Yeah.'

I asked, 'Would you like to pray about it together?'

John answered, 'Do you mind if I pray on my own?'

I said, 'Of course not.'

He said, 'Thanks, though.'

I said, 'It's fine.'

He said, 'No, really. Thanks.'

I think I'm going to cry now.

8.30pm

Mum says we really ought to be getting ready for bed.

John said, 'What for? I won't be able to sleep anyway.'

I said, 'Neither will I.'

Mum said it didn't matter because we'd still be resting and we'd need all our energy to carry on looking tomorrow. John asked if we could ring the police station again but Dad said there was no point. The policeman had taken all the details so if Gruff had been handed in they'd be sure to ring us.

I said to Mum, 'Please don't make us go to bed.'

She just said, 'There's nothing more we can do tonight. Dad'll pop up the road with the torch in a little while but there really isn't much point in him going far. Not till the morning.'

Not much point? How can she say there's not much point? Gruff's the most special dog in the whole world. And he's ours. If that isn't the point, I don't know what is.

8.45pm

Just brushed my teeth. Now my gums are bleeding.
They haven't done that for ages. The dentist always
says when your gums bleed you need to brush extra
specially hard because you're not getting them clean
enough.

I don't think it's that at all. I think they're just sad
tonight. Like the rest of me.

SUNDAY, 29 NOVEMBER
DON'T CARE WHAT TIME IT IS, JUST YAY YAY YAY-YIPPETY YAY!!

HE'S BACK! HE'S BACK! I don't think I've been asleep
all night but I don't care.

GRUFF'S BACK!!

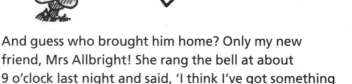

And guess who brought him home? Only my new
friend, Mrs Allbright! She rang the bell at about
9 o'clock last night and said, 'I think I've got something
that belongs to you.'

And there he was, all tucked up in her arms,
grinning away like he does, with his tongue lolling out.
He was quite muddy and his collar was missing. He'd
made Mrs Allbright's cardigan all dirty, but she didn't
seem to mind.

She said, 'When your mum said he was lost I thought, dear, dear, that won't do. So I decided to be another pair of eyes and ears.'

'Do you mean you went out looking?' John asked.

She said, 'I went out a few times. But the thing about dogs is they don't usually go far. Not if they know they're loved. I popped out just now and there he was trotting up the road on his way home.'

Dad checked Gruff over and he didn't seem to be hurt at all except for a scratch near his neck. What with that and his collar being missing, Dad said it looked as if he'd got caught up on something when he ran off. He must have been struggling to get free.

Poor, poor Gruff.

He was so excited to see us he kept sticking his nose in our faces and licking us. Mum said that was really yucky because we didn't know where his tongue had been. But we let him do it anyway.

Then Mum said, 'Right, first things first. He needs a bath.'

I said, 'Can Mrs Allbright stay and help?'

Mum said, 'If Mrs Allbright would like to, she'd be very welcome.'

Mrs Allbright said, 'Go on, then.' (You know, Mrs Allbright is the PERFECT name for Mrs Allbright, because when she's happy, her face really does go all bright and smiley.)

So Mum said, 'Right. You run the bath. I'll get the hot chocolate on.'

When we finally had to go to bed (we didn't mind nearly so much this time), John asked if Gruff could sleep with him instead of in the kitchen where he normally does. After all, he did need special care and attention because he'd just had a really bad day.

Then I said could I sleep in John's room as well, so we could all be in together because I'd had a really bad day too. Dad started to say, no, I couldn't, because I'd have to sleep on the floor. (I wouldn't have minded at all but parents can be really funny about stuff like being uncomfy.) But then Mrs Allbright said, 'I've got a camp bed under my stairs. Shall I pop home and get it?'

She is just SO cool!

In the end, Dad went and got it and set it up under John's window. Gruff spent the whole night snuggling up with John for a bit, then hopping off the bed and snuggling up with me. Then he'd go back to John, then come back to me, and on and on and on.

Saucy looked confused to start with but then she suddenly seemed to realise she had my bed all to herself. When I went into my room in the morning, she was stretched out right down the middle. She opened one eye when she heard me and looked at me as if to say, 'Get out! This is my room now!'

Think again, Saucepot!

9.30am

Just been talking to Mum about God.

I said, 'God really does listen to our prayers, doesn't He?'

Mum said, 'Yes, He does. Every single one.'

I said, 'He kept Gruff safe all that time. And, in the end, He made sure that the best person to find him was Mrs Allbright, because that gave her something to be happy about too.'

Mum said, 'Clever, isn't He? However He works things out, it's always for the very best.'

I said, 'When things aren't going right, it's so hard to remember that.'

She smiled and said, 'I know. For me too. It's not easy being a Christian, is it?'

I said, 'No, I suppose it isn't. Glad I am one, though.'

She said, 'Too right. No one else listens to me rattling on the way God does.' Then she saw the time and sighed, 'Oh, no, now we're going to be late for church.'

I said I was sure God wouldn't mind. After all, it's not every day we lose Gruff and find him again.

1.15pm

Something's happened to John. He came into my room. Which is normal. But he knocked first. Which isn't normal at all.

He said, 'Can I show you something quickly?'

I said, 'You can show me something slowly, if you like.'

He said, 'It's this.'

And it turns out he's made this FANTASTIC thank you card for Mrs Allbright. With a big piece of yellow sugar paper he had left over from his history project. He's

done a really cutesy picture of Gruff on it using stuck-on, chopped up crisp packets, like a collage.

I said, 'Wow, John, that is amazing!' (I wanted to ask, 'Where did you get all those crisp packets?' But I thought that would be a bit mean if he still wanted the stash under his bed to be a secret.)

He said, 'Thanks. I'm giving it to Mrs Allbright later. Do you want to come with me?'

I said, 'I'd love to.'

He said, 'Good,' and he started to go. Then he turned round and said, 'Sorry about when I wind you up and everything. I don't mean to. I sort of can't help it sometimes.'

I said, 'It's fine. You can't help being my brother.'

He said, 'Yeah. Anyway, you were really great yesterday.'

Then he went. AND he closed the door behind him. He NEVER closes the door behind him.

I've been sitting here with my mouth open ever since.

4.00pm

We've all just been out for a long walk with Gruff.

Dad said, 'Shall we let him off the lead?' and we all screamed, 'NO!'

I think he was joking because he gave a big grin. I hit him on the arm (only gently obviously) and then we started playing 'I Spy'.

I thought I had a really good one – I spy with my little

eye something beginning with G,P – but John got it straight away.

He said, 'Gruff's paws.'

I said, 'How did you know?'

He said, 'Because I'm better at being a genius than you are.'

Yup. Things are definitely getting back to normal.

4.30pm

Oops! I forgot to say – Sunday Club was brilliant this morning. Everyone was so pleased we'd found Gruff again – especially Louise, and she didn't even know he was missing in the first place!

She asked if we knew the story Jesus told about a shepherd who had one hundred sheep until one day he lost one of them. The shepherd was so upset that he left the other ninety-nine so that he could go and search for the one that had wandered off. When he finally found it again, he was over the moon. He picked it up, gave it a cuddle and carried it back home. Then he went and told all his friends and neighbours the good news.

Louise said, 'Jesus told that story to show how much God loves us. Even though there are lots of people like us who love Him and spend time with Him, it's not enough for God! He wants every single person to be His friend. But there are so many people who don't know about Him or don't really care. To God, all those people are like lost sheep. And Jesus is the shepherd who <u>so</u> wants to find them and bring them all close to Him.' Then she smiled at John and me and said to the others, 'Just think how excited John and Sarah must have been when Gruff came home. That's exactly what it's like with God. Every time someone says sorry to Him for the things they've done wrong, and every time someone asks to be His friend, God is <u>so</u> excited and happy. The trouble is that without God, people are lost like the lost sheep – or the lost Gruff! But when they say sorry to God, God finds them straight away.'

I told Louise I was keeping a diary now. She said, 'How fantastic.'

I said there was lots of stuff going on that I'd written down, but some of it wasn't sorted out yet.

She said, 'Don't worry. The important thing is that you're writing it. I'm sure that when you look back on it in the future, you'll be able to see exactly how God's been sorting everything out. That's how it works for me.' Then she said, 'It's like reading any good book. If you knew how it was going to end before you started it, there wouldn't be much point in reading it, would there?' And I think that's really clever.

She is SO brilliant and I'm SO glad she's one of our leaders. She's practising to be a teacher but she says it takes a very long time.

I said, 'I hope I'm still at school when you're a proper

teacher. Then maybe you'll be MY teacher.'

She said, 'I hope so too.'

7.30pm

I've just finished my letter to Gemma.

I said to Mum after supper, 'I still haven't done it.'

She said, 'Well, it has been a bit busy.'

I said, 'But I don't know what to say.'

She said, 'Just start by saying you're sorry and see what else comes out.'

I wanted to say, 'But supposing nothing comes out?' Only John was stuck on his homework so Mum had to go and help him because Dad was busy.

I sat down with a piece of paper and wrote down the being sorry bit, and after a while something else did come out so I wrote that down too. It goes:

Dear Gemma,

I'm really sorry about everything that's happened. I know we were talking about you in the library but it was only because we wanted to help. I heard the thing about your parents and I believed it. I shouldn't have listened, because it was up to you to tell me if you wanted me to know anything, not someone else. But I haven't been spreading any gossip about you, I promise.

So I'm sorry if I've upset you. I didn't mean to. I just want us to be friends again.

Love from Sarah

PS None of this is Josie's fault. It was me who was sticking my nose in, not her.

79

I wonder if she'll read it. I probably won't even give it to her. She thinks I'm a loser anyway.

In bed
I've just decided what I want to be when I grow up: Louise.

MONDAY, 30 NOVEMBER
Time to get up again
Why is it that on Saturday night I had a rubbish sleep and yesterday I didn't feel tired at all ... but last night I had a really good sleep and this morning I am SO tired?

I've just noticed something. I can't seem to pray for Charlotte Miller like Mum said I should. It's not that I don't want to (I don't think), I just can't.

Oh well. It's Charlotte's fault, not mine. She shouldn't have upset me so much.

7.30pm
Went round to Josie's after school. I wasn't going to stay long but her mum said I could have supper with them. So I rang Mum and she said that would be fine. We had jacket potatoes with sour cream dip – which John always says sounds disgusting, but it's not, it's really yummy. He's just boring for not trying it.

I told Josie about wanting to be Louise when I grow up.

She said, 'You can't really do that. You can't actually BE someone else.'

I said, 'No, I know, but I want to be as much like her as I can.'

Josie said, 'I wonder if that's all right.'

I asked, 'What do you mean?'

Josie answered, 'Well, Jesus wants us to be like Him, so perhaps we shouldn't want to be like anyone else.'

I hadn't thought of it like that, but I said Louise was probably a lot like Jesus anyway because she always seemed so kind and patient and caring and sensible.

Josie thought for a minute and said, 'Yes, so does my mum.'

Then I realised that MY mum does too, and my dad ... even JOHN can be those things some of the time – except maybe for the sensible part.

In the end we decided that when you're friends with Jesus, He obviously rubs off on you quite a lot.

I said, 'I suppose there'll always be bits of ourselves that could do with improvement, though.'

Josie said, 'Definitely. Are you still working on your life makeover list?'

I said I was, but number 8 (the one about not being shy of telling other people I love Jesus) is really hard. In fact I've been wondering about asking Mum if we could invite Mrs Allbright to church with us one Sunday. Then maybe I could try and explain to her why we go.

Josie said, 'That's a brilliant idea. I've been struggling with my number 5.'

Josie's number 5 turns out to be more or less the same as my number 3 – about needing to pray more. That made me think about the problem I had with praying for Charlotte Miller. It didn't help when I saw her in school today and she was still all smirky-smirky after last week. I didn't say anything to Josie, though.

I didn't want her to suggest something helpful like, 'Let's pray for her together.' I just wanted to do it quietly on my own. Sometime or other. Maybe not today.

Bedtime

Mum's been chatting to me about Gemma.

She sat on the bed and said, 'What's the news today?'

I said, 'There isn't any.'

She said, 'Did Gemma speak to you?'

'Of course not,' I answered, 'she's not even LOOKING at me now.'

Mum asked, 'Did you give her your letter?'

I said, 'No.'

She said, 'Why not? I'm sure she'll think it's nice of you to take the time to write it.'

I said, 'No, she won't. She'll think it's rubbish.'

Mum said, 'I really think you should just give it to her anyway. It might not make any difference at all. But at least you'll know you've done everything you can to put things right.'

Mum always says things that make sense. The trouble is, so far everything I've done has just made things worse.

Then Mum asked about Charlotte Miller. I said she was just irritating.

Mum said, 'You could always pray about that.'

I said, 'What, "Dear Lord God, please make Charlotte Miller less irritating"?'

'No,' said Mum in one of her you-know-perfectly-well-what-I'm-talking-about voices. 'You could ask Him to help you not to feel that way about Charlotte Miller.'

I could do, I suppose.

Maybe I'll give Gemma the letter tomorrow.

On the other hand, maybe I won't.

TUESDAY, 1 DECEMBER
8.00am (Countdown to Christmas!)

John seems to have got over being nice to me. He couldn't get in the bathroom when he woke up because I was in there washing my hair. I called out that I'd got up early specially. I wanted to start December feeling all clean and fresh. He said whatever I felt like, it didn't change what I looked like, so why bother?

I said, 'Thanks for that,' and made him wait an extra ten minutes.

Yummy chocolate in my Advent calendar – Christmas pudding-shaped. Last year, Josie and I had a competition to see whose 1 December chocolate lasted the longest. We waited until we were both sitting together on the bus, then we put our chocolates in our mouths at exactly the same time. The hardest part was just trying to let it sit on my tongue without doing any sucking or chewing. John said we were crackers.

I said, 'What, Cwistmas cwackers?' (I couldn't talk very well with a chocolate sitting on my tongue.)

John said, 'No. Nut cwackers.'

After school

No Charlotte today. Guess what? Now she's gone down with tonsillitis. I wonder if she's on the yellow death juice. Oh well. At least I didn't have to try and spend the day avoiding her.

Josie and I had a fantastic idea at lunchtime – well, it was my idea really, but we're going to do it together. I'd been thinking about how pleased Mrs Allbright looked when she found Gruff, and how happy Gruff was to be home.

So I said to Josie, 'If I can't be Louise when I grow up, wouldn't it be great to run an animal rescue centre? We could do it together.'

Josie said, 'What kind of animals would we rescue?'

I said, 'All kinds. We went to one last year and there were dogs, cats, rabbits, guinea pigs, ponies, even goats. We could give them all a really lovely home until they could be adopted.'

'Maybe we ought to go and live in the country,' Josie suggested. 'Then we could have fields and things.'

I wasn't sure about that, though. I said, if we moved

away, we wouldn't be able to go to Sunday Club any more. Josie pointed out that we'd be grown-ups by then so we wouldn't be doing Sunday Club anyway. And we'd find another church to go to. (I didn't much like the idea of going to a different church either. But I didn't mention it because I thought this was something we could talk about nearer the time.)

Then we drew out this amazing rescue centre plan. We're going to have our house in the centre so that we're living right in the middle of all the animals and can always see what's going on. The dog kennels can be at the back, with the cat ones at the front so that they're separate. That will mean we won't have lots of growling and hissing if they don't like each other. Hopefully we can have fields on both sides for the rabbits, guinea pigs, ponies and goats. We can build stables and wire runs there as well, so they've all got their own special places to go at night.

John came over at one point with a football under his arm and said, 'What's that supposed to be?'

I said, airily, 'It's our animal rescue centre, <u>actually</u>.'

He said, 'Poor animals,' and kicked the ball back to Dave.

Boys. They just don't have a clue.

Josie said, 'I wish we could start it now.'

I said, 'I know what we <u>could</u> do now. We could get some practice looking after different sorts of animals by looking after people's pets while they're away on holiday.'

I was really pleased with myself. Normally it was Josie who had all the ideas, not me.

'We'd have to start with small ones, I expect,' I added, 'like hamsters and mice, because we can keep them at home. Then, maybe when we're a bit older, we could do stuff like dog-walking. We could advertise … put a postcard in a shop window.'

Josie was REALLY impressed. She said I must have been thinking about all this for ages. (I hadn't. It had only just popped into my head.)

I said, 'Whatever happens, we DEFINITELY ought to work with animals. After all, God made them, so they're just as important as people.'

8.00pm

I tried to learn my spellings but they were so toe-curlingly boring I gave up and started colouring in our rescue centre plan instead. Josie said I could take it home because it was my idea, and also I wanted to draw some animals on it so it was more obviously a rescue centre.

I've just drawn myself holding out my hand to feed

a pony. It doesn't look much like me. Never mind. The pony doesn't look much like a pony either.

8.15pm
Mum's just got home. I expect we'll have to get ready for bed now. She's been out to an exercise class at the sports centre called 'Stretch Your Way To Fitness'. She saw it advertised on a poster when we were out walking Gruff last Sunday.

She says we only use a tiny number of our muscles doing everyday stuff. This means that all the ones that don't get used get really flabby and out of condition.

Dad said to Mum, 'I don't know why you want to go to something like that. There's nothing flabby about you.'

Mum said that wasn't the point. One of her resolutions at the beginning of this year was to get more exercise. So, if she started the class now, she'd just about get in four sessions before the next new year, which would mean she'd have kept to it.

'Besides,' she said, 'I don't want to wake up one morning in ten years' time and find that the flab's taken over.'

Grown-ups are so odd.

8.40pm

Mum's been in to say goodnight, but she says I can carry on writing for another five minutes.

She asked, 'Did you manage to learn all those spellings?'

I said, 'Mostly.'

Then she said, 'And how was Charlotte today? Still irritating?'

'Don't know.' I shrugged. 'She's ill.'

'Oh,' she said, 'that's a shame.'

'Yeah,' I said.

I <u>want</u> to feel that it's a shame, I really do. But somehow I can't. I'm still praying for Gemma even though she acts as if I'm an invisible sack of potatoes. But I just don't care about Charlotte Miller.

WEDNESDAY, 2 DECEMBER
After breakfast

Mum's limping this morning and every time she gets up, she seems to have to lean on something and hold onto her back.

John said, 'Mum, there's something wrong with your leg.'

Mum said, 'My leg's absolutely fine, thank you very much.'

John said, 'If it's absolutely fine then why are you limping?'

Mum said, 'I'm not limping.'

John said, 'You know all those muscles you were stretching last night that never get stretched? Perhaps you should just leave them alone to get flabby.'

Mum said, 'You know that breakfast cereal in the bowl in front of you? Perhaps you should just be quiet before you end up wearing it.'

4.00pm

I'm beginning to feel REALLY bad again and I don't know why. I'm not sure if it's because I haven't given Gemma the sorry letter, but I've got this horrible feeling inside.

What's even more weird is, after everything Charlotte did last week, it should be great her not being at school, but it isn't. I feel as if it's my fault she's got tonsillitis. It can't be because I've been better for ages and she's only just got ill. And anyway, if you've got bugs you don't go around deliberately giving them to people. It just sort of happens. I bet she thinks it's my fault, though.

Josie noticed there's something wrong.

She said, 'Why are you all grumpy today?'

I said, 'I'm not, am I?'

She said, 'Well, if this is you in a good mood, I'd hate to be around when you're in a bad one.'

I said, 'I can't help it if I don't feel happy.'

She said, 'You got Gruff back. WHY don't you feel happy?'

I said (actually I nearly shouted): 'That's the whole point. I DON'T KNOW!'

Even Mrs Parker said, when we were supposed to be tracing a map of the Isle of Wight, 'My goodness me, Sarah, what a long face. Put it away and get the happy one out.'

I HATE it when teachers do that. As if <u>they</u> never have bad mood days. It's SO insensitive. I mean, if you said something like that to them when <u>they</u> were being grouchy (which, let's face it, is quite often), your life wouldn't be worth living for at least the rest of the term.

Sometimes I don't think grown-ups understand that children are human beings too. Well, we are. And it's about time they realised it and stopped treating us like – I don't know – like … toy monkeys, or something. Even toy monkeys don't deserve to be nagged into looking happy if they don't feel like it.

4.20pm

I don't believe it, now Mum's at it.

'What's wrong with you, now?' she came in and asked – as if there's ALWAYS something wrong with me! And that is just MEGA unfair because I'm usually perfectly fine.

I said, 'Nothing.'

She asked, 'Is it Gemma?'

I said, 'No.'

She said, 'Is it Charlotte, then?'

I said, 'Why is it, whenever anything's wrong it

always has to be Gemma or Charlotte? Why can't it be something to do with getting a headache or having a sore toe? I just want to be left alone and for everyone to realise that there's more to my life than Gemma McKinley and Charlotte Miller!'

Mum smiled. 'Right.'

Then she limped out and shut the door behind her.

4.30pm

I honestly don't know which is worse – Mum telling me off for snapping at her, or Mum doing her calm and patient bit (like she's just done) and leaving me alone to carry on grumping in my own grumpiness. If she'd told me off I'd have felt bad, but because she didn't tell me off, now I feel bad anyway because I was nasty to her and she was nice to me.

Mums can make you feel SO guilty! If they'd only left you alone in the first place, you wouldn't have done anything wrong … because there wouldn't have been anyone there to snap at.

She's probably downstairs in the kitchen, waiting for me to come and say sorry.

Well, I'm not going to.

4.45pm

Just been down to say sorry to Mum.

She said, 'That's all right, sweetheart, would you like a jam tart?'

I said, 'Thanks,' and she gave me a strawberry one.

'How are your muscles?' I asked.

'Stretched,' she said.

8.00pm

I said sorry to God for snapping at Mum. Then I read my letter to Gemma again. It's awful. If someone gave me a letter like that, I'd probably want to sink it in a fishpond.

I wonder if Gemma is going back to Scotland. I really hope she's not. Mind you, since all she's doing is treating me like an invisible sack of potatoes, I suppose it doesn't really make a lot of difference.

THURSDAY, 3 DECEMBER
After school

Mrs Parker says the Christmas concert is going to be on 15 December, so we've got to start practising. She wants us to think of as many things as possible to do with Christmas so that we can put together a Christmas rap. Then she laughed and said that was a joke on the words 'Christmas wrap' (wrapping paper, get it?). I didn't think it was very funny, but Josie said that was because I was still grumpy. She said if Mrs Parker slipped on a banana skin while carrying her coffee and biscuits from the staff room, I probably wouldn't find that funny today. HA HA.

I managed to think of lots of Christmas stuff though: presents, crackers, candles, baby Jesus, Mary, Joseph, angels, shepherds, wise men, stable, Father Christmas, reindeer, camels, star, snow, robins, tree, decorations, glitter, cards, carols, mince pies, Christmas pudding (don't really like it but it's still Christmassy), elves, stockings.

Mrs Parker says that tomorrow we'll be getting into pairs to try and work out raps using all the ideas we've thought of. She says we only need to do a few lines per pair, but they've got to be really good because she wants to be able to use all of them.

Then, this afternoon, we were practising carols. We're doing 'Little Donkey' AGAIN this year. I think we've done it every year since I started school.

I whispered to Josie, 'Do you think we always do 'Little Donkey' because teachers think parents go "Aah, how sweet" every time they hear it?'

Josie didn't answer, she just carried on singing. So I whispered, 'It's not that I don't like it or anything, it's just that we do it every single year.'

Josie whispered back, 'Why are you still being such a grumpy boots?'

I was going to ask how wondering why we sang 'Little Donkey' every year was being a grumpy boots. But Mrs Parker made everyone be quiet so that she could say in front of the whole class, 'Sarah and Josie, will you please stop talking for five minutes and concentrate on the job in hand? Thank you.' (I thought that was really unfair because I'd been concentrating all afternoon. Also, unlike almost the whole of the rest of the class, I hadn't put my hand up once to ask to go to the toilet.)

Then we had to start again from the first verse. Josie looked really cross with me.

I thought, NOW who's being a grumpy boots?

After supper

I asked Mum if she liked
'Little Donkey' and she said,
'Yes, it's really sweet.'
Mmmm.

7.45pm

I wonder when this feeling's going to go away. Perhaps it never will. Perhaps I'm going to be one of those people who just feels sad most of the time but can't explain why. I hope not though. It makes you feel miserable being sad all the time.

8.00pm

This is so stupid! I really want to talk to someone but how can you talk to someone about something when you don't know what it is that needs talking about? I've asked God to take the feeling away, but it's still there. It just sits in my stomach like a lump of gone-off cheese.

I've been trying to take my mind off it by doing a bit of Christmas rap to show Mrs Parker tomorrow, but it's all rubbish. I hope Josie lets me be her partner. She's not very happy with me at the moment, though.

Oh no! Supposing Mrs Parker decides who we're going to work with. I might end up with Tom Gray – or, worse still, CHARLOTTE MILLER. Hopefully she'll still be ill. Not that I want her still to be ill, I just really don't want her to be my partner. I mean, how can you possibly rap with someone who hates you?

8.15pm

Just rang Josie. She says, of course she'll be my rapping partner and, no, she's not annoyed with me. She just doesn't understand why I'm in such a funny mood. I said that made two of us but I'd try really hard not to be tomorrow.

Then I said we had to tell Mrs Parker first thing in the morning that we were going to be partners. This would put an end to any ideas she might have of pairing me up with Charlotte Miller.

Josie said, 'Are you scared of Charlotte or something?'

I said, 'No, of course not. Anyway, I've got to go to bed now.'

That's it, then, I thought, I HAVE to be in a good mood tomorrow. So I've done it. I've put my letter to Gemma in my bag. If God wants me to give it to her, He'll have to show me a way to do it that won't be really embarrassing. I'll ask Him. And then maybe I'll feel all right again.

(Please, Lord God, let me feel all right again.)

FRIDAY, 4 DECEMBER
8.15am

I've got to go. I know I've got to go or I'll miss the bus. I just can't decide about this stupid letter. Supposing I give it to Gemma and it makes things even worse – not that that's possible! I mean, what could be worse than this? But what if she reads it and laughs, or reads it and then tears it into little pieces in front of me? Or tears it into little pieces in front of me without reading it at all?

I said to Mum after breakfast (quite casually, I didn't want to make a big thing out of it), 'I've decided to give Gemma my letter today.'

Mum said, 'Good for you.'

I waited but there was nothing else.

I said, 'Is that it? Don't you want to know how, or where, or when, or ... what I feel about it?'

She said, 'Sweetheart, if you want to give Gemma the letter, just do it. I think it's a great idea.'

Then she went off and started digging around in the freezer.

I was speechless. Parents! You <u>don't</u> want to talk and they won't leave you alone. You <u>want</u> to talk and they're more interested in frozen peas. What is happening to the world?

5.00pm

I can't believe John sometimes. He's just eaten tomorrow's chocolate out of his Advent calendar.

I said, 'You can't do that.'

He said, 'Why not?'

I said, 'Because it's not tomorrow yet.'

He said, 'So? It's not as if I'm changing the course of history or anything. Tomorrow will still be tomorrow whether I've eaten the chocolate or not.'

I said, 'I know that. I'm not stupid. But why didn't you wait?'

He said, 'Because it's Friday.'

Seriously weird – and one more reason I am SO glad I'm not a boy.

Anyway, I did it. I didn't say anything to Josie, I just did it on my own. I gave Gemma the letter.

Well, I didn't exactly give it to her. Not face to face. I sort of left it.

We'd been doing rapping. It turned out Mrs Parker wasn't bothered who worked with who as long as we produced something really snappy. So I had no problem pairing up with Josie. Gemma was the only one who didn't have a partner. Mrs Parker said she could work with Charlotte next week when she was better. But for now, she could get in a threesome. Only Gemma didn't want to. She said she was fine working on her own.

To start off, Josie came up with:

It's the time of year for doing all that Christmas shopping.
Santa's in his grotto, all around the elves are hopping.

I asked, 'Why hopping?'

Josie said, 'Because it rhymes with shopping.'

I said, 'I know that, but WHY would the elves be hopping? I mean, they wouldn't just be hopping madly around the grotto for no reason.'

She said, 'They could be excited.'

I said, 'Well, shouldn't we put that in?'

She said, 'There isn't room.'

I said, 'But otherwise it doesn't really make sense.'

She said, 'It doesn't have to make that much sense. It's a rap.'

Then I thought of:

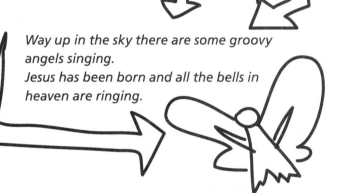

Way up in the sky there are some groovy angels singing.
Jesus has been born and all the bells in heaven are ringing.

(You have to say 'heaven' quickly otherwise it doesn't fit.)

Josie thought it was brilliant – which made me feel guilty for not saying her hopping bit was brilliant. But I just think that hopping elves are … well … sad.

We got sort of stuck after that, though.

I said, 'What about "Everybody's busy hanging up their decorations"?'

But then we couldn't think of anything to rhyme with decorations – at least not anything that was obviously Christmassy – so I don't think we're going to use that.

Anyway, when it was nearly the end of lunch, Josie

went to change her library book. I'd been thinking that if I hung around in the cloakroom, maybe I'd get two seconds in there on my own. Then I could stick the letter in Gemma's pocket.

And that's what happened. The bell went and I pretended to fiddle about in my bag, and suddenly everyone else had gone out. So I grabbed the letter, shot over to Gemma's peg and stuffed it in the pocket of her coat. I wasn't sure if I should leave a little bit sticking out so that she'd see it was there, but I thought someone might notice. I didn't want anyone else reading it.

Then, just as I was going out of the cloakroom, Gemma came in! She looked at me, then realised who it was so she looked away really quickly. But she did end up having to hold the door open for me. I think I must have gone red because my cheeks felt all hot.

At home time, I zipped out quickly so I could check if the letter was still there in Gemma's pocket and, guess what? It had gone! I think she must have found it almost as soon as I put it in there. I don't know if she read it, though. What shall I do if she hasn't? I don't know how else to say sorry.

I said to Mum, 'I gave her the letter.'

Mum asked, 'And are you feeling better?'

I said, 'I don't know.'

Mum said, 'Well, try and stop thinking about it. There's not a lot more you can do.'

I thought, yes there is. I can pray that Gemma will read it and know that I really am sorry. For everything. So that's what I'm going to do all weekend.

8.20pm

Just got back from youth club. Louise is SO AMAZING! Charlotte Miller is a lost sheep!

SATURDAY, 5 DECEMBER
7.00am

I'm so excited! I know why I've been feeling really off about everything.

Last night Louise said, 'Hi, Sarah, had a good week?'

I said, 'No, not really.'

She said, 'Why not? You didn't lose Gruff again, did you?'

I said, 'No, Gruff's fine. It's just …' And then it all sort of tumbled out.

I told Louise about Gemma and the big fall out a few weeks ago, and then the even bigger fall out last week, which was all Charlotte's fault. Then I explained about writing the sorry letter.

I said, 'If Gemma still doesn't want to be friends with me after she's read my letter, I'll never forgive Charlotte Miller. She's messed up everything.'

Louise didn't say anything for a minute, then she asked, 'And which part of all of that has made you feel the worst?'

'I don't know,' I said. 'Not knowing how to say sorry to Gemma, I suppose. And just wanting to be friends again.'

Louise asked, 'What about Charlotte?'

I said, 'What <u>about</u> Charlotte? She's been off nearly all week. She's got tonsillitis.'

'Have you prayed for her?'

'Why? It's only tonsillitis. She'll be back on Monday.'

Louise smiled. 'I think you might be missing the point.'

I said, 'Well, I'm certainly not missing Charlotte.'

Then Louise asked if I remembered what she'd talked about last Sunday.

I said, 'Of course. Lost sheep.'

She said, 'That's right. And who does God see as His lost sheep?'

I said, 'People. All the people who aren't friends with Him.'

She smiled again. 'Exactly. So what does that make Charlotte?'

That's when I got it! That's when I realised why I'd been feeling so down in the dumps. God wanted me to pray for Charlotte and I hadn't done it. I <u>couldn't</u> do it. She'd upset me too much.

I'd been able to pray for Gemma when she'd upset me, but with Charlotte it was different. Charlotte made someone else think badly about me and I couldn't forgive her for that. And because I couldn't forgive her, I couldn't pray for her either.

Louise says that sometimes God may want us to do something that we really don't want to do. Then, because we ignore Him and don't do it, we can feel bad inside. That's what's been happening to ME. Mum told me a week ago that maybe God wanted me to pray for Charlotte, but I didn't do it because I didn't want to.

I said to Louise, 'But what if I can't forgive Charlotte?'

She said, 'Maybe you can't. But God can – and you're on His team. So He can help you forgive her too. Then,' and she gave me a little shove, 'you can get on with praying for her, can't you? God doesn't want her to be a lost sheep for ever, you know.'

Isn't that incredible? I mean really AMAZINGLY, FANTASTICALLY, WOWZILY INCREDIBLE?

AMAZINGLY, FANTASTICALLY, WOWZILY INCREDIBLE?

So when I got home I had to go and pray really urgently.

I can't remember everything I said. I know I kept on saying sorry over and over and over again. I asked God to help me forgive Charlotte lots of times too. It was really strange, though. All of a sudden, in my head she didn't look like Charlotte any more. She really did look like a little lost sheep – all sort of sad and lonely.

Then I understood how unhappy God must be because she ignores Him, and how much He wants her to be able to find Him and be His friend.

So that's what I'm praying for. Charlotte pokes fun at Josie and me because we go to church, and I know she doesn't like us. But I'm going to keep asking God to help her to be friends with Him one day anyway.

8.30am (Just had breakfast with Mum)

I feel SO much better. That horrible, lumpy feeling in my stomach isn't there any more. To prove it, I ate FOUR Weetabix. Being on God's team is just the coolest!

10.00am

Phone rang while Mum was in the shower.

It was Auntie Jan.

She said, 'Gran's just fallen down the front steps and broken her leg.'

She sounded really upset so I went and got Dad. Dad said I'd better call Mum.

I said through the bathroom door, 'Mum, Auntie Jan's on the phone.'

Mum called, 'Can I ring her back?'

I said, 'I don't think so. Gran's just broken her leg.'

'WHAT?'

The shower went off straight away and suddenly Mum was hurtling down the stairs wrapped in a towel. She grabbed the phone from Dad, said, 'Jan, what's going on?', and stood there, dripping, while Auntie Jan gave her all the gory details.

It turns out that Gran's got a broken leg, a badly sprained wrist, a black eye and a slight concussion. An ambulance has taken her to hospital.

Mum had to sit down because she felt sick. Dad made her a cup of tea. He put three teaspoons of sugar in it.

I said, 'Dad, Mum doesn't have sugar in her tea.'

He said sugar helps if you've had a shock.

John said, 'Gran's going to be all right, isn't she?'

Dad said, 'Of course she is. Tough as old boots, that one.'

Mum sighed. 'If only she didn't live so far away. I'm not a lot of good to her here.'

Then she took a sip of tea and made a face.

She said, 'This has got sugar in it.'

'It helps when you've had a shock,' I said, wisely.

'Helps with what?' Mum asked. 'Rotting your teeth?'

Dad threw it away and poured her another cup.

5.00pm

WHAT IS IT WITH ME AND MY LIFE ANYWAY?

As fast as I get one thing sorted, something else has to blast its way in and wreck it all!

I was feeling REALLY happy. I was! I was thinking, it's all right now, it's all going to be fine. Then Gran had to go and have this stupid fall and now everything's 1,000 times worse than it was last weekend when we lost Gruff. (OK, losing Gruff was REALLY bad, but everything's got to be at least a HUNDRED times worse now.)

Auntie Jan's rung about 20 million times today, and when one call – one diddly little call – was Josie for me, Mum said could I be quick in case Auntie Jan was trying to get through! I mean, how many conversations can two people have about a broken leg?

Anyway, it turns out that Auntie Jan is going off to Paris until the end of next week. So Mum – OUR mum, who we need to be HERE – is getting the train up to Yorkshire tomorrow afternoon so that she can go and look after Gran.

I said, 'Yes, but who's going to look after us?'

Mum said, 'Dad's around after work and we'll sort out what's going to happen after school before I go. I'm not going to leave you on your own, am I?'

I said, 'But that's what you <u>are</u> doing. I don't want you to go to Yorkshire.'

She said, 'Well, I'm sorry, but I have to. Gran needs my help.'

I said, 'Why? She's in hospital, isn't she? There must be loads of nurses there to look after her.'

She said quietly, 'Sarah,' (she always uses my name when she's trying not to be cross) '<u>my</u> mum's hurt herself very badly. Now, think about her and think about me. And stop being so selfish.'

SELFISH! ME! I'M not the one packing bags and buying train tickets. I'M not the one leaving my children for a whole week when I shouldn't be. It's not me who's being selfish. It's Mum. And Auntie Jan.

Sometimes I could just scream, scream, scream, scream, SCREEEEAAAM!!

7.30pm

I said to John, 'It's all wrong, isn't it? Mum shouldn't be leaving us.'

He said, 'It's only for a week.'

I said, 'It shouldn't be for anything.'

He said, 'We'll be all right.'

I said, 'But why does she have to go?'

He didn't answer for a minute, then he said with a really serious face on, 'If we didn't live with Mum and she'd hurt herself, we'd want to go and be with her, wouldn't we?'

I said to John that wasn't the point.

Well it isn't.

Is it?

SUNDAY, 6 DECEMBER
5.00pm

Mum's gone. The train came and she disappeared off. Now there's just this big empty hole.

I've got some maths homework to do but I can't be bothered.

Louise gave me a cuddle in church this morning.

She said, 'Your dad's here. John's here. Your friends are here. If you need someone extra to chat to, give me a ring. And God never goes away. Just keep talking to Him. He'll look after you – and your mum. And He'll help your grandma get better.'

'Yeah,' I said.

'Anyway,' she went on, 'if you ask me, you're going to be so busy with all those prayers, PLUS praying for Charlotte and Gemma, the week will go by in a flash.'

I don't think it's going to, though. The train went at half past two. It feels like six years already.

8.00pm

I keep thinking about how horrible I've been.
I ought to add it to my life makeover list. Number 9: Stop being so horrible. In fact, I think I ought to put it in twice – number 9 AND number 10.

When we were at the station, I was crying and that made Mum cry too. Dad didn't look so good either. I know John wanted to cry, but he didn't. He stopped himself by biting his cheeks a lot. I could see him sucking them in.

I said to Mum, 'I'm sorry, I'm sorry.'

She said, 'You don't have anything to be sorry about.'

I said, 'Yes, I do. I've been so horrible about Gran.'

She said, 'No, you haven't. It's just been a bit of a shock. For all of us.'

I said, 'I love you, Mum.'

She gave me a tissue and tried to smile.

'I know,' she said. 'I love you too. And I love MY mum – which is why I've got to go and see her.'

8.15pm

Mum rang on her mobile.

She said, 'Just wanted to say goodnight. You'd better be saving all my bedtime cuddles for next weekend. I shall want every single one of them when I get back.'

I said, 'You're not cross with me, are you?'

She said, 'Whatever for?'

I said, 'Being horrible.'

She said, 'Sweetheart, it's forgotten. Don't worry about it any more.'

I said, 'I wish you were here.'

She said, 'I'll be back there very soon.'

Then I had to give the phone to John.

8.30pm

Dad came in to say goodnight.

I said, 'If you say sorry to someone and they forgive you, it's like starting all over again, isn't it?'

He said, 'Absolutely.'

I said, 'Is it like that with God too?'

He said, 'Of course it is. We all do things wrong. But as soon as we say sorry to Him, He says, "That's all right. Let's forget about it and try again."'

I said, 'So, as long as I'm really sorry, God won't think I'm horrible any more either.'

Dad said, 'I very much doubt God ever thinks you're horrible. Sometimes we do things that He doesn't like,

but He never stops loving us. He
never stops loving <u>you</u>. Nor
does Mum.'

I've been thinking about
when Josie said Jesus wants
us to be like Him. I think
most of Him must have
rubbed off on my mum.
She's the best person in the
whole world.

MONDAY, 7 DECEMBER
After breakfast
Mum rang about half an hour ago. She said she's fed
the cats and the budgie, had a shower and some toast,
and now she's off to the hospital.

I said, 'I miss you.'

She said, 'I miss you too. Don't be late for school
now.'

Don't care about school. Don't want to go. We're not
getting the bus, though. Dad's dropping us off so he
can go in and explain what's happened. After school,
I'm going home with Josie. Today and tomorrow John's
going back with Dave, then the rest of the week he's
going to Benny's. Dad's picking us both up when he
finishes work.

The animals are sorted too. Saucy will be able to take
care of herself, because that's what cats do. But Dad's
asked Mrs Allbright if she'd mind letting Gruff out in
the garden a couple of times during the day.

He told us she said, 'Oh, I can do better than that. I'll take him for a little walk in the park at lunchtime.'

John said to Dad, 'You did tell her she mustn't let him off the lead?'

Dad said, 'Don't worry. She knows what she's doing. She used to breed cocker spaniels.'

I said, 'I never knew that.'

He said, 'There's probably a lot we don't know about Mrs Allbright.'

I thought, yes, Mrs Allbright is the surprise lady.

6.30pm

Spoke to Mum on the phone. She said Gran was all stiff and sore and her eye looked really painful. I asked if it would make her feel better if we all came up to visit. I said we could leave right now and bring our sleeping bags. We needn't make any mess or noise. We could take her flowers and grapes every day and talk to her a lot so she didn't get bored. Mum said Gran was probably a bit too tired for lots of talking just at the moment, but it was very kind of me to offer.

What I really wanted to say was, 'Please can't you just come home now?'

But I knew Mum couldn't do that so there was no point.

7.30pm

Everything is so weird. The whole world's carrying on quite normally, but nothing's normal at all.

Charlotte Miller was back at school. She was in the cloakroom when I got in this morning. She looked up when I opened the door, but didn't speak to me. I didn't really feel like talking to her either today. But then I thought about lost sheep and remembered I was trying not to be a horrible person. Anyway, I knew I had to say something because God would want me to.

I said, 'Hi Charlotte.'

She said, 'Hi,' without really looking at me. Then she walked straight out and let the door bang behind her.

I thought, some sheep are obviously far more difficult to find than others.

The next person I saw was Gemma. Only the back of her, though. She was heading for the office and she didn't spot me at all. I was glad really. She'd probably read my letter, thought, how pathetic, and thrown it away. She might even have decided to do something worse than just throw it away. For all I know, she could have spent all weekend thinking up the nastiest way possible of getting rid of it.

Then I thought of something REALLY awful. What if that was why she was going to the office – to ask Mrs Trowbridge if she could stick it in the paper shredder thing! Maybe she wanted to listen while it got all chewed up and spat out the other end!

Oh well. Maybe it's for the best. If Gemma knew about Gran's fall and Mum having to go away, she'd probably just say, 'So? Stuff happens. Get over it.'

After break, things got totally embarrassing. We were supposed to be working on our Christmas rap. Josie thought we should have another go at the bit about decorations, which reminded me that we'd be getting our tree soon. That made me start thinking about home and how Mum wouldn't be there at the end of the day because she was a million miles away. I burst into tears and Mrs Parker said I could go and sit in the library with Josie for a while if that would help.

I wanted to say, 'Nothing's going to help. I just want to go to Yorkshire.' But as my eyes were in the process of spurting water uncontrollably down my face and I knew that any minute now my cheeks would turn all red and blotchy, AND the entire class had stopped rapping so that they could have a good stare (it's impossible to cry in secret in this place), I thought perhaps the library would be better.

Josie said, 'Your mum's only gone for a few days.'

'I KNOW!' I wailed. 'But it feels like for ever!'

She said, 'I suppose so. My mum's never gone away so I can't really say.'

I said, 'My mum's never gone away before either. I'm not letting her do it again, though. Not without me.'

Josie said, 'She might not have to go anywhere again.'

I said, 'Well, if she does, I'm definitely going too. If I'd gone this time, I could have helped look after Gran. Instead of which I'm stuck here trying to come up with some stupid Christmas rap!'

Josie said, 'It's not stupid. It's going to be really good.'

I said, 'The bits you write will be. Everything I do is rubbish.'

Then I told her about Gemma going to the office to get my letter shredded.

She looked very shocked and said, 'Did she really do that?'

I said, 'Well ... I don't know. But she might have done.'

Josie said, 'Only YOU could imagine something like that!' and told me I had to try and be more positive. She said she knew this wasn't going to be an easy week but just because Mum wasn't here, that didn't mean everything else was bad. I asked how would she know and she said she just did, all right?

Then, after lunch, I was coming out of the toilets when she suddenly appeared out of nowhere.

She hissed, 'Is it all clear in there?'

I said, 'What?'

She said, 'Is there anyone in there?'

I hardly had time to say, 'No, I don't think so,' before she shoved me backwards through the door. I nearly slipped over on the wet patch where one of the basins is leaking.

'What are you doing?' I said, NOT very happily.

'I told you not everything's bad,' she answered. 'It's Gemma.'

'What about her?'

Josie said, 'She just came up to me and asked me what's wrong with you.'

I stared at her.

She went on, 'She wanted to know why you were crying.'

I felt as if my tummy was going to fall out.

'You didn't tell her, did you?' I said. 'She's the LAST person I want to know. She'd probably laugh at me.'

Josie looked a bit confused but said, 'Of course I didn't. I just said you had some family problems.'

'What sort of family problems?' I wanted to know.

'I didn't say, did I?' Josie said. 'Anyway, the point is, Gemma spoke to me. She <u>asked</u> me about <u>you</u>. Don't you see what that means?'

I couldn't see what it meant at all. The last time Gemma had asked Josie about me, I'd waited all evening for a phone call that never came.

'It means,' Josie announced, 'that she's not ignoring us any more. She spoke to me and she wanted to know about you. You don't want to know about someone you plan to go on ignoring.'

OK, that was a good point. I'm sure I should have felt excited.

But today, I can't. Today all I feel is sad.

8.00pm

Thought I'd better spend a bit of time Christmas rapping as I'd wasted the entire rapping lesson sobbing in the library.

So far I've got:

The stars are shining brightly on the

freezing winter snow.

Santa's packing presents, it'll soon be time

to go.

Far off in a stable Mary's baby lies asleep.

The shepherds go to visit Him and kiss

goodbye their sheep ...

I'm bored now.

8.25pm. In bed cuddling my hot water bottle

Why does Gemma always have to ask Josie about me? Why can't she just ask ME about me? Does she think I speak a different language from her or something, and only Josie can understand me?

8.30pm. (Very hot)

When I see Gemma tomorrow I'm going to say, 'Floobel grom pinkwompit, Gemma.' And when she asks, 'What does that mean?' I'll say, 'Ask Josie. The way you usually do.'

TUESDAY, 8 DECEMBER
7.30am

In spite of Dad coming in last night saying, 'Sleep well,' and me answering, 'Ha ha ha!' – not to be rude or anything, but Mum has disappeared off and I do miss her like absolute nutso, so sleeping well is probably not to be expected – I did actually sleep amazingly well. I even feel hungry.

6.30pm

Mum says Gran's probably coming out of hospital tomorrow.

I said, 'Yay! Does that mean you're coming home?'

She said, 'Oh no, not yet. She's going to need a lot of looking after. It's not easy getting around with a plaster cast the size of a big chimney on your leg.'

I said, 'Mmm,' and tried not to sound disappointed.

When I was round at Josie's after school, we'd prayed for Gran together. I'd asked God to help me put her first and not keep thinking about how much I wanted Mum back with me. Josie said that was a really brave thing to pray. I said it was all to do with numbers 9 and 10, but could she please not ask me about them because when I talk about them I cry and I think I'm beginning to wear my eyes out.

Mum asked over the phone, 'How was school today?'

I told her it had been odd. For one thing, Mrs Parker was being nice to me all the time and kept asking me if I was all right.

Mum said, 'Well, that's good, isn't it?'

I said, 'Yes. But scary.'

Then I told her about Gemma. I was coming out of the library at morning break when I nearly bumped into her. She said, 'Hi, Sarah.' I was so shocked I couldn't answer.

Then, when I was putting my stuff in my bag to get ready to go home with Josie, she said, 'Bye, Sarah.'

I said, 'Oh, yeah, bye.'

I probably sounded really stupid. But when someone who hasn't spoken to you for weeks on end (and has obviously been hating the fact that you're even breathing the same air as them) suddenly starts talking to you, it's a bit difficult to come up with anything intelligent.

Mum was really pleased and said, 'How fantastic!

I told you God was listening to you. He's just been waiting to sort things out at the right time.'

I said, 'She only said hi and bye. That doesn't mean things are sorted out yet.'

Mum said, 'Yes, but it's a start. Just think, by the time I get home, you might have had a proper conversation.'

I said, 'I wish you were home now.'

She said, 'I know, sweetheart, but look on the bright side. It's Tuesday. At least I'm missing my exercise class.'

After supper

Dad says I look very tired. I said it's not that, it's just that my eyes keep leaking so that I look as if I haven't slept for three years.

John said, 'The whole of your face looks as if it's been leaking.'

I said, 'Well, the whole of YOUR face looks as if it's been sat on by a gorilla.'

Now I've got to do my maths homework. Ooh, I'm so excited.

8.30pm

I've been thinking about Gemma. I suppose that was really quite incredibly amazing her saying hi and bye today. Maybe she didn't shred my letter after all. Maybe she'll have spent all this evening trying to write back to me. When I get in to school tomorrow, there'll be an envelope on my desk with three

pages of flowery notepaper inside (I don't know why but I just imagine Gemma having flowery notepaper) explaining everything and begging me to be her friend again.

I thought I'd better pray about her so I said, 'Thank You, Lord God, for Gemma's hi and bye. If possible, could she please say something else tomorrow like, "How's it going?" or "You know that maths? Did you manage to do question 6?" Sorry I haven't been excited. I just really miss Mum. Oh and by the way, please help Charlotte to find you so that she's not a lost sheep any more.'

When Dad came in to say goodnight he said, 'Try and stop those eyes leaking. It's Wednesday tomorrow. Mum'll be home soon.'

I said, 'Yeah. I'm glad you haven't gone away too. Night night, Dad.'

Night night, Mum.

WEDNESDAY, 9 DECEMBER

7.55am

I said to John in the bathroom, 'If someone hadn't been speaking to you for about a million years and then, all of a sudden, out of the total blue, they did, would you speak to them first the next day, or would you wait and see if they were still speaking to you?'

He said, 'I'd probably speak to them first, but that's because I'm a boy.'

I asked, 'What's being a boy got to do with it?'

He said, 'Boys don't fall out. They just go and play football.'

I thought he deserved to get wet so I flicked water at him with my toothbrush.

6.15pm

I can't believe it! I mean I honestly and truly just CAN'T. I've been saying thank You to God every five seconds. (Josie says I probably don't need to thank Him quite as often as that, but just saying it once doesn't seem enough.)

IT'S HAPPENED! After all the really bad stuff that's been going on with me and Gemma, finally I think it's sorted. And it's God who sorted it. No one else could have done.

I was in the cloakroom first thing. I didn't even see Gemma come in, but then I heard her say, 'Hi, Sarah.'

I said, 'Hi, Gemma.' She was standing by her peg a bit sort of awkwardly and I didn't know if I ought to say something else. But then some Year 4 girls came in and they were being all giggly in a corner, so Gemma went out.

I thought, if only they could have found somewhere else to hang around and giggle, we might have been able to move on to the 'How's it going?' bit. As it was, we were still stuck saying 'hi' to each other.

At least, that's what I thought. But I was wrong. When I went out, Gemma was waiting near the door.

She said, 'Can I talk to you at break?'

I said, 'Yeah.'

'Meet you in the library, then.'

'Fine.'

Josie happened to come out of the classroom at that moment. She said my eyes were all wide and staring as if someone had stuck them open with superglue.

I whispered, 'She wants to meet me.'

Josie asked, 'Who? Gemma?'

'Who else?' I said.

She asked, 'What do you think she wants?'

I said, 'How do I know?'

She said, 'Will you tell me later?'

I was going to say, 'Of course I will,' but then I thought, supposing Gemma wants to tell me something really private and makes me promise not to breathe a word to anyone ever?

I said, 'I'll tell you if she wants to be friends again. But if she tells me anything secret, I won't be able to tell you that. I mean, it would be like gossiping, wouldn't it?'

Josie didn't say anything for a moment. I wasn't sure if I'd hurt her feelings. But then she nodded and said, 'Will you tell Gemma I'm her friend too?'

'Definitely,' I said. 'Anyway, she may just be going to say, "I still think you're horrible and will you please stop writing me tragic letters."'

Hope it's Mum.

6.50pm

Yes, it was Mum. Had a chat with her first, then spoke to Gran. She's home now. She said it was hilarious trying to get the plaster cast with her leg in it into the taxi. At one point she thought she might have to lie down on the back seat with her leg sticking out of the window!

Mum sounds heaps happier and said Gran was looking much, much better. I said, could I tell her my good news? She said, 'I'm all ears,' but I didn't get very far because suddenly she had to go. Apparently Gran had managed to climb <u>up</u> the stairs without any help, but now she was stuck and didn't seem able to get back down again. So Mum said she'd ring back later.

7.45pm

I wonder what it's like to be in shock. I said to Josie after school that perhaps that's what I was in – shock.

She said, 'Why?'

I said, 'Because my mind seems to have gone all wizzy-dizzy and I can't seem to think straight.'

She said, 'That's normal for you, isn't it?'

I said, 'I don't think I'll ever feel normal again.'

GEMMA'S MADE UP WITH ME!

The first thing she did when I met her in the library at break was to take my letter out of her pocket. I thought, right, this is it. She's going to give it back to me and say it's the most pathetic thing she's ever read.

But she didn't at all. She said it was the nicest letter anyone had ever written to her. She said she didn't deserve it because SHE was the one who ought to be saying sorry for being so nasty.

I said, 'You haven't been nasty.'

She said, 'Yes, I have. I was going to try to talk to you on Monday, but then you were crying and Josie said you had family problems, so I thought I'd better leave it.'

'Not problems, exactly,' I started to say.

'It's all right,' she went on, 'I know about family problems. And I just want you to know if you need anyone to talk to, you can talk to me.'

I said, 'Thanks.' (I was so shocked I couldn't think of anything else.)

Then we had one of those silences – the really awkward ones where you're both just sort of sitting there hoping the other person's going to say something, but they don't. So you start fiddling with your finger-nails and wishing the bell would go or that there'd suddenly be a fire practice – you know, any excuse to leave.

In the end Gemma said, 'What Charlotte's been saying about me is true. My parents are breaking up. Well, they've broken up already. My dad's moved back to Scotland.'

I felt as if my mouth was going to drop open and I had to force it really hard to stay shut.

'He told us he was going on bonfire night,' she sighed, 'but he actually went the day after.'

My mouth did drop open then, and there was nothing I could do about it. It was after bonfire night that things had all gone wrong and Gemma suddenly didn't want to have anything to do with me any more.

I said, 'Gemma, that's so awful! Why didn't you tell me?'

She said, 'I couldn't. I didn't want anyone to know.'

It turns out that Gemma and her parents had moved house so many times already that, when they came here, she'd almost decided it wasn't worth making any new friends – after all, she'd only have to go through all the upset of leaving them again when her mum and dad decided they wanted to go somewhere else. But she met me and we got on so well she couldn't help being friends.

Then her dad moved out and her mum said she and Gemma would probably go back to Scotland too, so she just thought, what's the point? If she didn't have any friends here there'd be no reason to be sad about leaving. So she stopped being my friend.

I said, 'If you'd just told me what was going on, I'd have understood.'

She said, 'I didn't want to tell anyone. I didn't want anyone knowing anything about me. I just wanted to be able to move away without people noticing I'd gone.'

I said, 'Did you really think I wouldn't notice?'

Then, of course, the bell had to go and ring so we had to get back to class. Staying in the library talking to Gemma was obviously much more important – especially as we were only going to be practising Christmas rapping – but I didn't think Mrs Parker would see it that way.

Gemma said quickly, 'Charlotte found out about Mum and Dad because her mum works with my mum, but I never thought she'd start telling everybody. Then, when she said you were in the library talking about me, I thought maybe you were spreading it around school as well.'

I said, 'I wasn't, I promise. I wouldn't do something like that.'

She said, 'I know. I knew all the time really. And when you wrote me this letter I thought, I can't go on not saying anything. I've got to explain it all to you – especially NOW.'

I said, 'What do you mean?'

She said, 'Family problems. If you've got them too it makes it easier to understand someone else's.'

I felt really bad then. My mum's gone but only because Gran needs her, and anyway, she's coming back at the weekend. It doesn't sound as though Gemma's dad is ever coming back.

We didn't see each other at lunchtime because

Gemma was doing art club.

Then, at home time she said, 'We're all right now, aren't we?'

I said, 'Of course we are.'

She said, 'See you tomorrow, then. You can talk to me whenever you want.'

I need to tell her about Mum and Gran. I hope she's not sorry she told me about her dad when she knows my family thing isn't like hers.

8.45pm. In bed

Chatted to Mum again for ages. John said if I didn't stop talking soon I'd end up with my tongue in a plaster cast like Gran's leg because it would wear out and end up snapping in the middle.

I said to Mum, 'Do you think I ought to pray that Gemma's parents get back together?'

Mum said, 'I think you need to pray that whatever happens will be for the best for Gemma and her mum and dad. What we think is the right thing isn't necessarily what God thinks is the right thing – and He sees it all so He's the one who really knows.'

I said, 'I didn't think about it before, but Gemma's a lost sheep like Charlotte, isn't she? If I pray for God to find her, He'll help her to be all right because, wherever she moves to, He'll be there with her. Then she'll never need to feel she's on her own.'

8.55pm. Still here

Dad says I've got to lie down now.

I said to him, 'It must be horrible to have to live without your dad.'

He said, 'You mean you'd rather I was here even when I nag about you leaving your shoes in the lounge or losing the remote for the TV?'

I said, 'Yeah.'

Definitely yeah.

IN THE WAY!

THURSDAY, 10 DECEMBER

7.30pm

Fab day! Fab day! Just such a

FANDABBY-DABBY DAY!

Managed to tell Gemma first thing this morning that my family problem was nothing like as huge as hers, but when I told her what it was, she was really pleased. Not really pleased that Gran had hurt herself and Mum had gone away for a week ... no, she said she was really sorry about that. What she was pleased about was that my parents weren't breaking up.

I said, 'It doesn't mean I don't understand how awful things must be for you. I know you must miss your dad like mad, because I miss Mum like mad and she's only gone for a few days.'

She said, 'I know, it's fine. Honestly.'

PHEW! That's something else off my mind.

Then she hung out with Josie and me all lunchtime. It was wet so we had to stay in, and we asked Mrs Parker if we could put our two separate Christmas raps together to make one long one that we could perform all three of us. Mrs Parker said that was a brilliant idea and she'd much rather see children working together than by themselves. And Gemma wasn't keen on pairing up with Charlotte Miller (Charlotte didn't care. She was giggling away with a couple of her friends.).

Gemma's rap was really good and we practised until the bell went. We worked out different moves we could do as well. Then Josie said we ought to think about costumes. Gemma suggested maybe we should just bundle ourselves up in Christmas wrapping paper and pretend to be parcels. I couldn't stop laughing.

I was still laughing in history.

Mrs Parker said it was nice to see me looking cheerful again, but there wasn't a lot to laugh about in London during the Plague, so would I mind saving my giggles until after school?

I did try. I didn't manage to, but I did try.

At home time, Josie and I were just about to zoom off and get the bus when Gemma caught us up and asked if we'd both like to go back to her house after school tomorrow! Like,

I said to Josie on the bus, 'Can you believe this? I've been praying about it for SO LONG. I'd started to think God didn't want Gemma and me to be friends.'

Then Josie had one of her brilliant ideas. She said why didn't we go back to Gemma's after school tomorrow, then all three of us go on to youth club afterwards. Then maybe, just maybe, we'd have a chance to talk to her about God. I mean, Gemma knows we go to church and everything, but we've never actually talked about it. And after all, trying to tell people about Jesus is number 8 on my makeover list. Just imagine if I could talk to Mrs Allbright AND Gemma – and maybe even Gemma's mum – and they all ended up coming to church with us and being God's friends too! That would be just SO cool!

8.20pm

Told Mum everything on the phone and she said, 'Do you remember when this all started and I told you you needed to be patient? Well, maybe that's what God's been teaching you: patience. He does listen. He listens to every word, but sometimes He just wants us to learn to wait.'

I said I wasn't very good at being patient but she said it didn't matter, she wasn't very good at it either. The important thing is that I hadn't given up and I hadn't stopped praying. I'd even ended up praying for Charlotte Miller as well.

'I know it doesn't seem like it some of the time,' Mum said, 'but God really does have a plan for us. We just have to wait for Him to do things when He's ready, not when we want Him to.'

It's still a pain Gemma's moving back to Scotland.

8.30pm. In bed

I am SO not sleepy. I wonder if I've still got that shock thing, because all the wizzy-dizziness hasn't gone away from yesterday.

Saucy isn't helping. I've given her loads of fuss already but every time I stop scratching her tummy, she grabs onto me with her claws and it really hurts! It's also quite hard to write with a cat hanging off your fingers.

Now she's trying to eat my pen. I wonder if all cats are barmy.

o oops

I've been praying about tomorrow.

I said, 'Dear Lord God, thank You so much for sorting everything out with Gemma. I'm sorry I wasn't patient. Please let her want to come to youth club. And if a good time comes up to tell her about You, help me to know exactly what to say. Help her to find You so that she's not a lost sheep any more. Then even when she's not with her dad, she'll know that You're right beside her and that you're her Father in heaven every day.'

FRIDAY, 11 DECEMBER
7.30am
Mum rang really early.

SHE'S COMING HOME TOMORROW!! YAAAAAA-AAAYYY!!

Auntie Jan's flight from Paris gets in at about 9 o'clock this morning so she'll be with Mum and Gran by lunchtime. And Gran's getting on so well she reckons she won't need someone with her all the time soon anyway. Mum says she absolutely flies around on her crutches and it's difficult keeping her away from the hoover.

There's a train that gets in here at 5 o'clock tomorrow evening and Mum's going to be on it! I can't wait! Dad says we'll go out first thing in the morning and buy a Christmas tree. Then we can get it all decorated and everything looking Christmassy as a surprise for her when she gets home.

I hope Mrs Parker's in a good mood.

HOW ON EARTH AM I SUPPOSED TO CONCENTRATE ON ANYTHING TODAY?

After breakfast

As soon as I see Gemma this morning, I'm going to ask her about youth club.

Collect the set:

Know God's help every day
Gruff and Saucy's
Topz-turvy Tales
ISBN: 978-1-85345-553-7

You can always talk to God
Dave's Dizzy Doodles
ISBN: 978-1-85345-552-0

Confidently step out in faith
Danny's Daring Days
ISBN: 978-1-85345-502-5

Become a stronger person
John's Jam-Packed Jottings
ISBN: 978-1-85345-503-2

Keep your friendships strong
Paul's Potty Pages
ISBN: 978-1-85345-456-1

You can show God's love to others
Josie's Jazzy Journal
ISBN: 978-1-85345-457-8

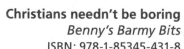

Christians needn't be boring
Benny's Barmy Bits
ISBN: 978-1-85345-431-8

Make new discoveries about God, yourself and your life as a follower of Jesus

TOPZ FOR GIRLS

Ever dreamt of writing your own mag? Giving your friends a makeover? Designing your own dream bedroom? And how well do you really know yourself - and God? Find all this (and much more)!

Topz Secret Diaries: Just for Girls - Special things about me
ISBN: 978-1-85345-597-1

TOPZ FOR BOYS

Fancy yourself as a footballer? Spaceship designer? Could you run your own TV channel - and, if so, what would you show? And how well do you really know yourself - and God? Find all this (and much more) inside!

Topz Secret Diaries: Boys Only - Stuff about me
ISBN: 978-185345-596-4

For current prices visit www.cwr.org.uk
available from CWR or Christian bookshops

IF YOU LIKED THIS BOOK, YOU'LL LOVE THESE:

TOPZ

An exciting, day-by-day look at the Bible for children aged from 7 to 11. As well as simple prayers and Bible readings every day, each issue includes word games, puzzles, cartoons and contributions from readers. Fun and colourful, *Topz* helps children get to know God.
£2.85 each (bimonthly)
£15.50 UK annual subscription (six issues)
Prices shown are correct at time of printing

TOPZ FOR NEW CHRISTIANS

Thirty days of Bible notes to help 7- to 11-year-olds find faith in Jesus and have fun exploring their new life with Him.
ISBN: 978-1-85345-104-1

TOPZ GUIDE TO THE BIBLE

A guide offering exciting and stimulating ways for 7- to 11-year-olds to become familiar with God's Word. With a blend of colourful illustrations, cartoons and lively writing, this is the perfect way to encourage children to get to know their Bibles.
ISBN: 978-1-85345-313-7

For current prices visit www.cwr.org.uk
available from CWR or Christian bookshops